ONE WAY OUT

Book 1

CARA BROOKS

ISBN:

978-0-9958172-0-3 (Book)

978-0-9958172-1-0 (Electronic Book)

To my dear
longtime friend
Dawn!
Carol Stojan

AKA CARA BROOKS

I would like to dedicate this, my first novel to DD ANDER, who inspired
me for almost a year as he wrote his first, then his second novel.
He demonstrated his joy of writing and dedication day by day.
Finally, I could bear it no longer and was compelled to begin my own novel.
Thank you Duane, for your encouragement and ongoing mentorship.

I would also like to thank my family and friends for encouraging and
supporting me always, in my writing endeavours. Especially I want to thank
my late father, Dr. Frank J. Stojan for his ongoing love and support for the
whole of my life. This one is for you Dad.

Preface

IF ROBERT HAD been more attentive to his wife's unhappiness and palpable sexual resistance, he might not be slumped over the green chair in the attic tonight. But then again, life is more complicated than that, isn't it?

As an accountant, who worked out of his home, Robert was gifted at numbers and minutiae. Not so great at the big picture view or relationships though. One really cannot be faulted for their natural shortcomings, can they? Read on dear reader. You decide.

Chapter 1

Casey

CASEY FELT GUILTY yet excited as she turned the key, locking her writing room attic door, from the outside. Grabbing her coat, keys and purse, she raced out of the house and jumped into her blue Volvo. *Oh my God, I did it!* The surge of vitality she now felt had been absent from her inner world for months. The howling wind energized her in this moment of euphoric clarity. She backed out of her long driveway, turned left and headed for the West Coast highway, leaving her husband behind, in the attic.

For many years, Casey's work as a compassionate yet no-nonsense counsellor, filled her head with other people's problems, allowing her to sidestep her own. It had served her well until recently, when she quit counselling to write full time, planning to return to University for a Master's in Psychology. This major transition prompted Casey to realize that living with Robert was not healthy for her. *If he'd been more understanding and less defensive this may have turned out differently. But I know him, he would never have let me go, not ever. Obsessive-possessive sex addict,* she silently called him. *Does anyone's life turn out as expected?*

Casey was a fresh faced, lean, attractive thirty-two year old brunette, who was perplexed by the unraveling of her marriage in recent months. Although she was aware that her own reactions had contributed to the situation, she felt that Robert had changed in the past year. Finally, after weighing all the facts, she took responsibility for her contribution to the discord and decided to act tonight. *I hope I'm not losing it, this is so out of character for me. I'm usually the rational one with a splash of impulsivity, to make life interesting. Maybe that is only relative to Robert's off centre behaviour this past while. My actions tonight might be extreme, but I have my reasons. His being an accountant and working from home means I had to get creative if I wanted to leave him without warning. Lately it seemed, he never left the house.* Casey had counselled many women on how to plan a getaway, carefully and safely. She had been slowly preparing to leave Robert, if and when she'd had enough. *Good thing he isn't a police officer like my first husband or I might never have had the courage to act.*

Now, driving along Highway 101 on the gorgeous west coast of Washington State, Casey looked at the panoramic view and sighed. *This drive is mesmerizing and a beautiful testament to hope. Some people would call this running away, but I call it running towards my new life. I'm so thankful that I was able to get away tonight.*

I now understand and empathize with those who lose it and hurt their partners. One truth that no one talks about is we all have a dark side within us. Anyone can be pushed to their limit if circumstances become difficult enough. Sadly, I now know this to be true.

She feels her own dark side and knows that it must to be dealt with. Robert's anger within the marriage had somehow transferred itself to her. She would never have imagined herself drugging, then locking someone in an attic. *Yes, we all have a dark side,* Casey cringed.

As the highway darkened, Casey felt anger surge through her again. She had been having night terrors that he would hire a hit man to kill her. An unimaginable thought until recently. She had met some of his unsavoury friends who were, in Casey's mind, capable of doing just that. *Not a great way to live, thinking someone might be gunning for you. It turns out you really can judge a person by the company they keep. Locking Robert in the attic probably wasn't the best idea though.*

On the day I married him I was so certain we would be together forever. It was a beautiful moment when I believed our destiny was to share our lives. Life is rather like an ever changing sea, it swells, ebbs and flows, calming and frightening yet we are ever drawn to it, with hope or despair...our choice.

She took a deep breath and looked across at the vast ocean. With the sun going down and gorgeous purple sky glowing over the breathtaking seascape, Casey slowly began to feel less agitated. A thread of exhilaration wove through her now and again. *I will get excited about life again. Happiness is having a tank full of gas, an open road and the freedom to go. All I need to do, to escape the heavy oppression of Robert, is take back the reins of my life. Thank you God for giving me the courage to leave today.*

Casey turned off the highway, in pursuit of a quaint seaside resort called Kalaloch Lodge near the Olympic National Park in Washington State. It was recommended by a friend and when she found it online, it looked so appealing and serene; she decided that would be her first stop. *I don't even care if I get lost trying to find it. This scenery is so soothing and beautiful.*

The longer she drove the better her outlook became. The tension of her sustained inner conflict was diminishing and she felt relaxation enveloping her body and mind. Suddenly an animal darted out in front of her car. She held the steering wheel as best she could, but instinctively she pulled to the right, heading for the cliff, which dropped off sharply towards the sea. Her hands tightened on the wheel. Two thoughts flicked through her mind. *Is this payback for locking Robert in the attic? Is this really how my life is going to end?*

Chapter 2

Robert

Robert's body didn't move for some time, after Casey drove off. Finally, he stirred and opened his eyes, waking up from the alcohol mixed with a sedative. His head was aching as he checked his watch. Groggily, he calculated he must have been out of it for a couple of hours.

Where's Casey? What's going on? He stumbled to the closed door and tried to open it. *Why the hell am I locked in here?* Robert was instantly furious, desperate to get out of the attic and more desperate to find his wife. He hollered through the door.

"Casey get up here! Casey?" Nothing. No sounds from down-stairs. *I better find something to get this door open.* He kept rubbing his aching head as he hunted for a tool or instrument to break through the door. Still feeling drugged, his movements were slow but determined. Robert was never one to give up and he wouldn't now, no matter how lousy he felt.

Gradually his mental fog started to clear as anger rushed through him. He remembered how Casey had created the illusion of a romantic evening, here in her writing room. It was her favourite space in their rancher and he had been touched when she invited him up here, on their anniversary tonight. He thought she wanted to make amends. But now, he knew that it was no accident, locking the door from the outside. Robert was getting madder by the minute. *How dare she lock me inside!*

The fight yesterday was really minor compared to some of their blow ups. It started because he wanted to have sex before the dinner party. Casey always had one excuse or another but he knew that once he got her going, she would get into it. Which is exactly why he always persisted when he wanted to have sex. He knew her better than she knew herself, he told himself. Yet last night, she really dug in her heels and refused. Flat out no. Robert decided he wasn't going to let her get away with that. He had one of his raging headaches and she knew that having sex helped alleviate them. So he told her to go ahead and refuse but do not expect any money this month to put towards that education fund. Casey was saving up to go back to University and finish her Master's Degree. This was important to her and Robert knew it. So she succumbed, once again, to his pressure. Robert had no idea how much Casey resented these scenarios. All he knew was that he got what he wanted.

What he didn't know was that he had finally pushed her too far. Robert shook his head. He had no idea Casey had the gumption to pull off something like this. One tiny part of his brain admired her maneuver but he was still angry. Actually very angry, as he kept hunting for something to break the lock or door. He opened up another box and he spotted a heavy metal anvil.

"This might do it." He said out loud.

With great difficulty he hauled it out of the box. *This could be too heavy for me to lift high enough to smash into the doorknob. I'll get it swinging, if I can. That might work. Under different circumstances this could have been a fun game, a sex game.* He smirked to himself as he heaved the anvil up. *This heavy lifting must be working off some of my anger. I will get out of here, find Casey, buy her a new coat or purse and we will be good.* Robert was gifted at denial.

She treats me like an imbecile half the time. So why shouldn't I get lots of sex, I deserve it for putting up with her superior attitude. It's her duty anyway. Why else would a man get married and stay with only one woman?

"*Seriously!*" He muttered to himself.

Robert struggled to heave the anvil but it was very awkward to get a decent grip. He turned it over and grasped it from another angle. *There, that's better.* He heaved it upward and got it swinging then he took a crack at the door knob. It smashed the knob off but the lock was still intact.

"Brilliant move Einstein...what's your next genius idea?" That swing took just about all he had, for the moment anyway. He sat down to take a breath and think.

Robert was an intelligent, attractive, well built man with a strong jaw which Casey had always told him had attracted her from the first. He always took good care of himself. Bordering on obsessive, some might say. His office was immaculate and he always knew what he wanted, when he wanted it. But in relationships, his motto was 'do nothing and most problems will disappear'. At least that was what Casey often told him was his MO (modus operandi). He prided himself on that tactic, actually. He believed women in general could do well to practice it. He'd often joked about writing a book himself, on that very topic.

Right now though, he was frustrated and confused. He decided to take another swing at the door and see if he could break the lock. *Damn you Casey! If this is your idea of a joke, I'm not buying it!* Robert heaved the anvil up once more and swung as hard as he could at the door with a huge bang. He didn't hear the car outside, pulling into his driveway.

Chapter 3

Casey

"I'm not going out like this!" Casey muttered. She reefed on the wheel, jerking it left and then held it steady as she finally took a breath.

"Oh my God, I didn't go over! Thank you, thank you!" Casey pumped the brakes and collapsed over the steering wheel as the car came to a stop. She was shaking. Humbled by the thought that she almost died, in fact, would have died had she not turned the wheel, she started to cry. She had never felt so vulnerable in her life. Gratitude swept over her and she suddenly felt huge regret for locking Robert in the attic. *What was I thinking? He could die up there. Have a heart attack trying to escape!*

Without thinking it through any further, Casey decided she would return home to make sure Robert was okay. She owed him that. Death looming so close had given her a certain perspective. Not once did it cross her mind that she might be in shock. As the chills set in, Casey cranked up the heat in the car, then carefully turned the car around and started driving back. Yes, she was definitely in shock now, though she didn't realize it.

The relaxation that had been setting in just before her near accident, had completely dissipated. Now, she was beginning to wonder what she would have to be deal with when she got home. She thought about her marriage.

I loved Robert when I married him. We respected each other, had lots of laughs together and great sex. Robert had always been quick to anger, but in Casey's experience, most men she had dated, were. However, in the past year, things had changed between them. He started getting bad headaches which had been investigated. Nothing was found so the doctors prescribed pain medication and simply told him to return if they got significantly worse. That is when Robert started pressuring her for constant sex. It seemed as though each time they had sex, Casey wanted to savor it while Robert was already talking about how soon they could have it again. Her previous enjoyment was replaced by resentment. As a result they were not connecting. The situation was making her feel out of control and angry most of the time, which was not like her. *I know you shouldn't blame someone else for how you feel, but that IS how I feel, controlled and diminished by Robert's needs.* Even thinking about it could fill Casey with a rage she was unaccustomed to, before Robert. *Thank you Robert for getting me in touch with my dark side, which I never even knew I had.* She said to herself sarcastically.

As Casey drove along the darkening highway, she began to hope she could get through to Robert perhaps reach a mutual under-standing. Her chills were going away but now she was truly anxious about seeing him. *I just need to make sure he is okay.*

Casey sighed and shifted her attention to her surroundings. The light was gone except for the moonlight cloaking the sea like a rippling ribbon. *The sea is so breathtaking. I am so grateful to be alive. I will check on Robert and explain why I need to be away from him.* Casey had no idea what was in store for her. If she had, she wouldn't be going back now.

Chapter 4

Robert & Casey

As Casey turned into her driveway, it looked like Robert was still in the attic, by the lack of lights on the main floor. Just as she opened the front door, she heard a huge bang!

"Whoa! What was that?"

She hurried into the house. No sign of Robert so she went directly to the stairs leading up to the attic door. It was still closed.

"Robert! Are you okay?" Casey called out.

"What the hell? Casey, let me outta here, now!" He banged hard on the door with his fist.

Oh oh! He sounds really mad. What am I going to say to him? She began to second guess herself. *How about the simple truth? I will just try to reason with him.*

Casey called out "Robert, I'm going to unlock the door now."

"Dammit Casey, hurry up!" Robert yelled.

Casey hesitated. She was a jumble of nerves. She exhaled, then turned the lock and pushed the door open. An enraged Robert lunged at her, knocking her backwards, down the five steps. She was caught off guard and had no time to grab onto anything. Down she went, hard, landing on the hardwood floor at an odd angle. Casey was a tall girl so when she hit the ground, it is a hard hit. She wasn't moving. Robert rushed forward, a surge of adrenalin flushing his body.

Although still enraged at her, he could see that she did not look good. He knelt by her side.

"Casey? Are you okay?" Nothing. But she was breathing.

Robert stood up and went to hunt for his cell phone. He cursed under his breath for letting Casey talk him into giving up the house phone and use only cellphones. He raced into the kitchen, it was nowhere in sight. *Did she hide it, so I couldn't call anyone once I got out of the attic? Was that why she insisted on giving up the house phone originally? Has she been planning this all along?*

"Now I'm really getting paranoid!" He grumbled out loud. *And why did she lock me upstairs, leave, and then come back? What gives woman? You're acting more like my mother everyday. And trust me, that's not a compliment!*

He raced into the bedroom, looked around but didn't see it. He stood there thinking. Then walked over to his night table, opened the drawer and there it was. He quickly dialled 911 as he rushed back to see if Casey was awake yet.

As he came around the corner, it was clear she had not moved. The 911 operator was now asking for details. He hurriedly gave her the pertinent facts, stating his wife had fallen down some stairs.

"It was an accident, hurry!" The operator told him to stay on the line, an ambulance was on its way. Robert hung up the phone. He had to think. How would he explain this? He knew from watching crime shows that he would immediately be a suspect. *Little do they know, I was the victim here, but who will believe that story?*

He heard the ambulance siren, getting closer and decided he would go with simple accident when they asked. The main thing was to get Casey looked after. He knelt down beside her again, trying to waken her. Still no response when he called her name.

The Medics pounded on the door. He ran over and opened it for them. They had a stretcher and asked him to step back to let them take over. By now Robert was on the verge of losing his cool. After his time stuck in the attic, now worried about Casey and possible repercussions, he was getting testy.

"Tell me what's happening! Is my wife okay?" He practically shouted at them.

"Getting upset isn't helping buddy." The male medic replied while the female medic shot him a dirty look.

They were putting a neck collar on Casey; had her on oxygen now and she was still not responsive.

Robert took a breath and apologized. "Sorry. Can I come in the ambulance with her?"

"No, we want you to follow behind. Thanks." The male medic was firm. Robert didn't argue. He figured he better not make any waves now.

Chapter 5

Robert

*H*alf an hour later the ER Doctor came out to speak with Robert.

"I understand your wife took a fall down a short set of stairs. Is that right?" He asked.

Where is this going? Why doesn't he just give me the goods? He checked himself. He did feel guilty. *But hey, she started it.*

"Yes Doc she fell accidentally." *Am I being too obvious? I've been in jail for assault and there is no way I am going back there. Casey or no Casey!*

"Was this the result of an altercation?" The doctor probed.

Now Robert was getting steamed. *But I better not show it. Breathe, stay cool.* He warned himself.

"Not a chance Doc. Tell me is she awake yet?"

"Your wife is non responsive yet her vitals are stable at the moment. She is in a coma. We have scheduled her for an MRI of her brain and spinal cord so we can determine the extent of her injuries." Before Robert could say anything the Doctor continued. "The police are just arriving now and would like to talk to you."

Immediately defensive, Robert yelled "What exactly is your problem Doc? My wife fell and now you're telling me she is in a coma with God knows what! Then on top of that nightmare you are sending the police after me!" Robert's cool was gone.

"Mr Paterson, this is strictly hospital policy. All such injuries must be investigated, especially when one party cannot speak on their own behalf. We are simply trying to protect the injured party." The Doctor excused himself as two police officers approached Robert.

Here we go. Be smooth, confident and friendly. Robert fixed an innocuous smile on his face.

After introductions the officers took Robert aside to speak in private. *Who knew the hospital had a space for questioning?*

The older officer took out a notepad, "Please tell us exactly what happened before and after your wife fell. We need your statement now. When your wife wakes up, we need to confirm your story."

Meanwhile both officers are staring right through him, as if they could read his mind. *I guess this is the latest tactic of crime investigation, mind reading.* Robert thought sarcastically. He tried to stay calm.

"She had arrived home then she ran up the stairs to the attic where I was just coming out the attic door. We collided and she went down."

Robert wanted to stick to the truth as much as possible. That was one tip he had picked up in jail. Along with 'always lie with confidence, never succumb and you will be believed'. He knew this to be a proven fact. *Those suckers who believe that truth will always come out, are dead wrong. I am proof of that.*

"Then what happened?" The officer probed.

"Umm I checked on her then looked for my phone to call 911." Robert felt nervous but hoped it didn't show. He was perspiring now.

"How long would you say it was before you called 911? Ten minutes, half hour or longer?"

Oh hell, what are they getting at? "I'm not sure, maybe ten minutes. Why?"

They ignored his question. "Then what happened?"

"What happened? Nothing happened! I called 911 and you know the rest!" His voice was getting louder.

"Not so fast Mr. Paterson. After you called 911 what did you do?" The 2nd officer was getting involved. He was more abrupt with an aggressive stance.

"Ummm I think I just checked on Casey again. I tried to wake her."

"You think? Did you or didn't you check on her?" The 2nd officer stared at him.

Robert ran his hands through his hair, a nervous habit. "Yes officer. I checked on her. Then the ambulance arrived."

"So, what do you do for a living Mr. Paterson? How long have you two been married?"

"What does that have to do with anything?" Robert was ticked.

"Just answer the question now or we will have to take you down to the station for formal questioning." Officer 2 just wouldn't let up. *Is he trying to provoke me?* Robert was full of questions but not getting any answers.

"Okay okay... I am an accountant. I work from home. We've been married three years." Robert tried to be polite. *This is going from bad to worse. I need to get it back on track. Stay chill.*

"What happened this evening before your wife fell?" Officer 1 joined the conversation.

Robert took another deep breath. "We had been celebrating our anniversary until my wife ran out to pick up something. Why?"

"What was the 'something' she went out to pick up?" Officer 2 was getting aggressive again.

"Look officers, I am done here. I am worried about my wife and I cannot even think straight right now. Thanks." With that Robert turned to leave.

"Hold up mister. We aren't done until I say we are done. Like I said, we can either do this here or at the station, your choice." Officer 2 sounded as annoyed as Robert felt.

Chapter 6

Casey

Casey is trying to figure out what that whirring noise is. It's so loud. She cannot open her eyes, or move her body. Raging headache too. Finally the whirring stops. She has a sensation of moving, then hears voices.

"This poor woman. Her husband probably did this."

"Ya, the guy seems a little touchy. Men! What are you gonna do?"

"Okay let's get this gal back to her room. I will send the report as soon as the radiologist has taken a look and finished it. See you soon."

Casey tried to put the pieces together to make sense of what was happening. But she was feeling so tired.

Next time she 'woke' she heard a man say her name. "Casey, can you hear me? Casey?"

Yes. I can hear you! But she could not speak or move. Her head hurt and she wanted to go back to sleep.

Chapter 7

Robert

The officers wanted to know Robert's life history, it seemed to him. Now the previous jail time had come up. *This is not looking good.* Just as he was about to lose it again, the doctor came by. He asked the officers to step aside so he could update Robert on Casey.

"Your wife has suffered a severe concussion. We are trying to stop the swelling so we will keep her in a coma until we feel it safe for her to come out of it. As well, she has a spinal injury. We need to operate to relieve pressure on her spinal cord but cannot do so until we get the swelling down in her brain. At this point it becomes a wait and see, day by day scenario."

Robert said "Will she be okay doc?"

"It's not possible to say yet. She's young and fit but it really is too soon to tell. I will update you with any changes." The doctor started to walk away.

"When can I see her?" Robert was getting frantic. This was all out of his control and he didn't like it. *Casey has to be okay!*

"First things first, Mr Paterson. The police need to finish up with you now."

Both officers walked back over. Robert started to feel dizzy. He just wanted this nightmare to end, now. After another round of questions, the officers cut to the chase.

"Did you and your wife have an argument? You seem like a guy who doesn't have a good handle on your temper. Come on, did you knock her down the stairs?" The 2nd officer smirked at him.

Robert couldn't control himself any longer. He took a swing at the officer which barely made contact.

"Whoa! Hold it right there!" The 1st officer grabbed Robert by the shoulder, spun him around and got out his cuffs.

"Okay, let's go. Now! You need to have some time to cool down mister!"

Robert was so mad now he could have killed the guy. *That officer deliberately goaded me, just so he would have a reason to take me in. I'm not a complete idiot.*

As they drove to the police station, the 1st officer informed Robert that due to his assaulting a police officer, they were going to keep Security outside Casey's room. He would not be permitted to see her until she was able to confirm Robert's version of events. Robert was livid!

"So typical of you guys. Railroading an innocent man while you let the real crooks out there go free!"

Chapter 8

Casey

Casey was fortunate as the swelling around her brain went down relatively quickly. Two days after her fall, she woke up and finally got her questions answered. The doctors told her that she required surgery on her spine immediately.

The police officers came around just before her surgery to get her statement. Although embarrassed to tell the whole truth, she did. Due to the fact that Robert had assaulted the officer, they understood that his aggression was why Casey locked him in the attic, in order to leave. They chose not to charge her for that action. Robert didn't either, so she was relieved.

It was clear that Robert's volatile temper played a big role in what happened and the officers asked her if she wanted him charged for assault. Casey was torn. Because of her training and her general nature, she was very compassionate and preferred not to get Robert in trouble. But the deciding factor was that, without an assault charge, there would be no Restraining Order.

"Yes officers, go ahead. I know how obsessive he has been lately, so I will not feel safe unless he is ordered to stay away." She thanked them. Then she was wheeled off to surgery.

Her surgery was successful. Then the rehabilitation started. Everyday day was pain and hard work as Casey slowly got her legs working again. She had been told it could have been worse so she tried to stay positive and grateful. A natural optimist, she was able to keep her spirits up, most days and even those of her fellow patients going through similar struggles. Robert had been sentenced to five months in jail. She could only imagine how angry he would be. *I feel bad for Robert and guilty for my part in it, but his aggression is really what landed him in jail.* Like most women, Casey had an inclination towards guilt. But she also had a good degree of self awareness and managed to keep her emotions in balance now that she was away from her destructive marriage. Everyday she thanked God that she had finally gotten away from the dark energy which had been seeping into her. Her anger towards Robert was slowly subsiding.

The hospital stint gave Casey lots of time to ponder her life. She thought about her parents, who were gone now. Her childhood, from outward appearances, looked perfect. But of course, no childhood is. Her father was a minister and her mother was a part time librarian. From her father, Casey learned kindness and compassion; while her mother was more of a detail person. As Casey observed them growing up, she had always admired her father's life of helping others. Her mother seemed unhappy much of the time and was overly critical.

She probably was unhappy as she lost a child and perhaps never grieved properly, Casey, the adult, surmised. Tommy, Casey's little brother had died in a bike accident when he was seven years old and Casey was ten. It was not an easy time for any of them. Casey recalled wondering why her father could not comfort her mother, as he comforted so many others.

Now of course, Casey understands that many couples struggle with the death of a child and often the marriage doesn't survive. Her family stayed intact, yet it operated as broken. In her teenage years she spent as much time away from home, as she could get away with. *No wonder I ran off and married at the age of nineteen, only to discover that my husband was far more controlling than my mother.* She smiled at her youthful naivety. *When you're young, you simply cannot see how each choice will affect your life forever. But then again, you learn from every mistake. Two failed marriages later, I must be pretty smart,* she mused.

She was feeling good today, in spite of everything. Her doctor had told her she was getting strong enough to go home any day now.

Casey had a plan for her future and was determined not to let anything stop her. *I just need the doctor's release and I will be on my way. I cannot wait to get going and start the next chapter of my life, before Robert is released.*

Chapter 9
Robert

Robert was hatching his own little plan, from behind bars. Firstly, he was a model prisoner. He wanted early release on his five month sentence. *The sooner I get out of here, the sooner I can convince Casey that divorce is not an option.* He had been served with divorce papers which he ignored. Secondly, his headaches were getting worse. He had considered trying to escape on one of the two hospital trips since his incarceration. But in the end, decided not to be that stupid. *That's making a bad situation worse. I'm not going to tempt myself with that idea. It's not worth it.* The doctors never did find a cause for his headaches and they were getting worse, so he was living on pain killers.

Chapter 10

Casey

Casey was excited. The plane would be landing in Dublin within 20 minutes. She was finally getting on with one of her major dreams. To go to Ireland and write. This past year had been a rugged one and now she felt like the ugly past was behind her.

Robert got five months for his assault on Casey, but got out in four months for good behaviour. A Restraining Order was in place to keep him away from her. He was released a week after Casey got discharged. She was quite sure he would come looking for her. So when she got discharged, she immediately went back to their rental, took her basics then stayed with a girlfriend. She continued with her physical therapy, made her travel plans and now here she was with a new grateful lease on life. She still had scars, both physical and mental to deal with but she was hoping Ireland would be a healing environment for her.

What she didn't know was that Robert had been watching her for the past few weeks. Definitely a breach of the Restraining Order. He knew the day she got on the international flight. He just didn't know where she was headed, yet.

Chapter 11

Casey

It was a drizzly day when Casey walked out of the Dublin Airport to grab a cab. The cool misty air hitting her lungs was a welcome infusion. While listening to the rapid Irish brogue surrounding her, she felt a bit disoriented. She could barely understand much of it due to the rapid speech of English mixed with Gaelic.

I will get an ear for it eventually, she told herself. Her mobility was still on the slow side displaying her vulnerability, so she did her best to walk with a strong stride. Having been married to a cop when she was young had taught her a few things. One of which, was that a woman should always walk as though she's very strong. It will help deter a crime being enacted against her. *I was so naive and malleable when I was nineteen. Anything he taught me about safety is ingrained in me forever. And that is all good. I wish I had been more cautious with Robert. I won't make that mistake again.*

The friendly cab driver came across as a decent guy and introduced himself as Fergus. Casey gave him the address of the cottage she had leased online. It was so appealing in the pictures she couldn't wait to get there. She just hoped it wouldn't be a huge disappointment. He said it was about a forty five minute drive.

Hopefully it's not too isolated. The landlord told me I could walk to get groceries, so how bad could it be? I'll rent a vehicle if I need to. Casey told herself.

As the car weaved along the curvy roads, the city was left behind when the luscious green countryside opened up. She could barely believe the beauty before her.

Ahhh...this is what I have been dreaming of. This beautiful countryside is a feast for the eyes and a balm for the mind. I am really here! She sighed contentedly as she realized how stressed she had been the past while. *Travelling has its challenges too, especially if your mobility isn't the greatest.*

Soon, another little village appeared. Lots of old buildings made with stone and brick. There was charm oozing out everywhere. *I love this,* Casey thought.

"We are almost there. This is the shopping neighborhood closest to your address." Fergus offered.

The small cobblestone street had a handful of brightly colored shops and one very prominent pub with an old sign which read Flanagan's, which made her smile. Casually dressed people were everywhere. *No high heels around here,* she noted. *This is my kind of town!* That was just one of the things Casey liked about being a full time writer, no need to project an image.

"It's very charming." Casey said to Fergus.

"Here we are!" He said as he pulled into a gravel driveway. The rain was still coming down so Casey pulled her hood over her shoulder length brunette hair.

The Cottage exterior was exactly as the pictures had shown. Lots of green trees and shrubs with neighboring houses not too close. *It looks so inviting!* Casey was really fired up now. Tuckered out yet energized, she imagined her future at this cottage.

As she stepped out of the cab, a tall man with dark curly hair walked by accompanied by an adorable Schnauzer-like pup. Casey was a borderline obsessive dog lover. She loved all breeds, all sizes, it didn't much matter. When the small dog spotted her, it came tearing over with tail wiggling and jumped at her legs.

"Rachel! Come!" The man called. Rachel stopped, looked back at him, then jumped back at Casey, tail wagging.

"I'm really sorry. She is still being trained." He said in a deep voice with mild Irish accent.

Casey could understand him easily.

"It's really okay! I love dogs. She's adorable! How old is she?" Casey asked as she bent down to scratch Rachel's ear.

"She's five months now. Quite an energetic bundle for sure. Loves her walks." He stated.

"Well, you're a lucky guy. I still miss my little dog. They really get into your heart don't they?" She smiled. *This is one attractive man. Stop it Casey! He's got to be taken. Besides girl, you are nowhere near ready for a man,* she chastised herself.

He walked over and leashed Rachel. "It looks like you're renting the O'Grady place. Welcome! We won't keep you. Cheerio!" With that he and Rachel continued on their walk.

That was a nice welcome. Maybe he's a friendly neighbour, let's hope so.

She turned her attention to her driver who had already put her suitcases on the front steps.

"Thank you very much!" then handed him the fare plus a tip. She stood on the little porch and waved him off before hunting for the hidden key. After he drove off she looked around once more to be sure no one else was walking by or watching her, then lifted the end brick away from the bottom edge of the steps. *There it is, in the plastic baggie, exactly as he said. Thank goodness. So far, so good.*

"Now for the rest of the story." She said out loud.

She put the key in the lock, turned it and the door popped open. Dark inside, Casey reached for a switch. It took a bit before she found one- then light!

"Oh my!" Casey said out loud as she looked around the room. *It is even more inviting than the pictures,* she thought with relief.

There was an old fashioned fireplace, with wood stacked beside it. Two love seats, one on either side of the fireplace facing each other. There were two standup lamps, both Tiffany style, beside each love seat and hardwood flooring as far as she could see with an area rug for comfort. Also a smallish square wooden dining table with four wooden chairs.

Perfect! She thought. But best of all, was a writing desk positioned against the large window overlooking the back garden.

"I think I just arrived in heaven!" Casey said out loud.

How did I ever get so blessed? I cannot wait to begin writing here!

She turned and realized she had left the door open with her bags outside. She walked back and retrieved her two suitcases. After closing the door, she noticed it didn't close properly unless she locked it. *I'm okay with that. It's a good safety precaution. I will never accidentally leave my door unlocked. It's good.*

She continued her tour through the chilly house noting the earth tone colors, her favorite. *I love these colors which is partly what caught my eye, online. That and the charming garden out back. Completely private, like a sanctuary,* she smiled to herself.

The kitchen was old and tiny but functional. *Good enough. Kitchens are not my thing anyway, so who cares?*

The bathroom was adequate and rather roomy Casey thought, for the small size of the cottage. The master was cute and charming with one large window overlooking the garden plus two corner windows which would give daylight all day long.

The den was especially inviting with another desk and one wall lined with books. *This place was made for a writer!*

Casey took another hour or so to get a fire going and settle in. When she crawled into that comfy bed she promptly fell asleep, feeling more at peace than she had in a long time.

Chapter 12

Robert

Robert was trying to decide when to make his move while also congratulating himself for going on a hunch about ten days before his last night with Casey. He had noticed her getting testier each day, so he had put a tiny GPS tracker inside her favorite suitcase. The one she referred to as her 'travel buddy' and often said she couldn't live without. He knew her history of running away from relationships and decided he best cover himself, just in case.

So now he knows exactly where she is. He also knows there is no restraining order against him in Ireland. He's decided to go over there so he can watch her and formulate his plan to get her back. *She's my life and there's no way she's staying out of it. Actually living overseas will be better anyway. We can start afresh over there.*

He had given notice on their rental property and moved their furniture into storage; then emailed his clients that he would be on another extended leave. As a self employed accountant, it would simply appear that he was 'living the good life' he told himself. *No one needs to know I was in the clinker,* he chuckled. *It's a good thing we didn't buy that house we were looking at. Prices are a lot lower in Ireland. Good pick,*

Casey. Ever the realist, Robert was. Besides his fantasy of getting Casey back, he also had no knowledge of how difficult it is to purchase a property in Ireland and what a long process it can be for foreigners.

Within two days after Casey's departure, Robert boarded a plane to Dublin. He had been to Ireland twice before. *My stories about that green lush country are probably what inspired her to go there.* Her GPS indicated that she was not on the move. *This might be easier than I thought. I'm sure she misses me as much as I miss her, by now.* At least, that is what he told himself.

Chapter 13

Casey

While Robert was in the air on his way to see her, Casey was getting acquainted with her new surroundings. On this, her first morning, the sun was shining which was especially appealing after the downpour the night before. The back garden was fresh and alive with moisture. She could not wait to get into the garden and check out each plant and tree. But first she needed to get the cottage functioning. Groceries were the first activity on her list. Exploring her new world was a close second.

She stepped outside, got her bearings in the daylight and headed towards the shops, only to be surprised by the man and his dog Rachel. Once again the pup came bounding up to greet Casey.

"Good morning to you young lady!" He called out.

"Young lady? Me? Why thank you." She smiled at him. *This guy is way too cute. Mr. Blue Eyes.* She thought silently.

"Anytime!" He gave her a lazy grin. "How was your first night at the O'Grady place?"

"Basically perfect." Casey replied. "Then to wake up to this unexpected sunshine is more than I could have hoped for."

"Well, make sure you enjoy it now, because it may not last." He grinned. "Hi, I'm Adam."

As Casey grasped his hand, she felt a spark go through her. "Oh hi! I'm Casey. Great to meet you, my very first acquaintance here, not counting the cab driver or Rachel." Casey could not get the silly grin off her face. *It's been a while since I felt like such a girl!*

"It's not likely the last time we will run into you. Rachel and I go for a lot of walks. It does both of us good as I work out of my home so I need fresh air or my brain goes numb!" Adam said. "You're an American?"

"Yes, sorry about that. I know we are not the most popular people overseas. It's kind of embarrassing to admit, frankly." Casey blustered.

"Oh no, I didn't mean anything negative at all. Some of my favorite relatives live over there. My parents!" *This is one attractive girl and I don't want to offend her.* "Besides, you are not your government right? I mean, you don't work at the White House do you?"

"Heavens no! What a nightmare that would be! I am a writer." Casey reluctantly offered.

"Really? I won't ask you what you write. I know how that feels talking to a virtual stranger, trying to explain your genre. I too, am a writer. One day maybe we can do coffee, tea or beers and have a real discussion."

"Oh thank you for not asking. Of course, you would get that. Umm, sure I would like that, one day." Casey said awkwardly, not wanting to appear over eager, yet wanting to be honest. She bent down to scratch Rachel's ears again to hide her flushed face.

"I'm off to the Main Street to get some basics. I guess I'll be seeing you around." When flustered, the easiest out was to escape, Casey's MO.

"Sure. See you. Come on Rachel!" Adam continued his walk.

Casey walked the other way, thinking *what an interesting man. Friendly too.*

The shops were only about a four block walk from the cottage. As she approached the food store, she decided to stroll along the two streets first and take an overview of what was there. Then get groceries and head home. She still felt a bit 'displaced' in this foreign land with the new dialect drifting to her ears but she found the fresh air plus sunshine, most welcome. Being outside had always been Casey's favorite place to be. Nearly all her best childhood memories took place in nature. *Given the beauty here, no wonder I was drawn to Ireland. I am so relieved to be here now, away from the past.*

As she sauntered in front of the shops she noticed people were looking at her. *I suppose I don't look Irish. Plus, in a small community like this, everyone probably knows everyone.*

When she got to the corner, she stepped off the cobblestone and walked onto the road to cross over to the other side. Just then, a motorcycle came tearing around the corner and nearly crashed into her. A tall blond muscular man quickly stepped forward and pulled her back, just in time. But she took a tumble backwards and fell, just as he grabbed her.

"I'm so sorry miss! Are you okay?" He asked.

Casey felt embarrassed. Normally she would have been able to jump out of the way, but with her recent surgery she was definitely slower to react. As she lay on the ground, she was afraid to move when she felt the pain in her back.

"Oh please don't apologize! You saved me! I should have been more careful. I feel so silly." She looked into his dark eyes.

He was staring at her. "Are you all right miss?" He asked again. "You look like you're in pain. I'm a doctor. Where does it hurt?"

"My back hurts. I had back surgery four months ago. I hope I haven't damaged anything." Casey was still looking into his eyes.

"Let's take a look. Just lie still." He proceeded to check her limbs, very slowly lifting her legs, one by one. When he lifted her left leg Casey yelped out in pain.

"I think we need to get you to the hospital and just make sure you haven't injured anything. What was your surgery?"

Casey explained as best she could without too much detail. "They operated on a lower vertebrae, as I took a fall and one was pressing on my spinal cord. They needed to relieve the pressure."

"Okay, I'll call an ambulance just to make sure we don't hurt anything further moving you."

He is definitely a take charge kind of guy. I cannot believe I did this!

After chatting in the ambulance, it turned out that Dr. Hawthorne, or David, as he insisted she call him, was from Seattle. Not very far from where Casey lived. Crazy how you meet people so close to home when you go half way across the world. Casey immediately trusted him and felt comfortable.

When they got to the hospital David stayed with her. He insisted. "I feel somewhat responsible. If I'd pulled you out of the way more carefully, you might not have needed to come here. Let's just see what is going on."

Casey had also told him she had just arrived at the O'Grady place last night. So he knew she was alone. *Maybe he just doesn't want me to be on my own, dealing with a hospital in a foreign land. I'm certainly getting the royal treatment. All the nurses seem to be falling all over themselves helping Dr. Hawthorne.*

An hour later, her X-ray results came back. She was fine. Her injured area had just been bruised and as it wasn't 100% healed yet, she would have to let it settle down again.

"Thank goodness! I'm so relieved I haven't damaged it again."

"Yes." David said. "You are lucky. The doctor will come back and give you a prescription for anti-inflammatory medication. You will be fine in a week or so, if you take it easy."

"Oh I will. I know how much fun it's not, to be unable to walk. Believe me, I'm a good patient. I have learned the hard way, to always follow doctor's orders." Casey teased him. She was taken aback at how easy it was to be with David. *I feel like I have known him forever. It must be his bedside manner. Life is one crazy surprise after another. Maybe it's just the pain meds they gave me.* But she was glad David was there.

After the Doctor came by to release her and give her two prescriptions, one for pain and one for inflammation, David wheeled Casey outside to his car.

"I can stop at the Pharmacy and get your meds for you okay? Also do you need anything else picked up? It's probably going to be a number of days before you can get out again."

Casey was reluctant to ask for his help. *But he is offering,* she told herself.

"To be honest, I was going to get groceries to stock up. I have cash. If you have time, would you be able to pick up a few things for me?" Casey was feeling very tired now.

"No problem at all. I'd be happy to." David responded enthusiastically. *He really does seem to want to help. I am rather a damsel in distress and he is stepping up, that's for sure.*

Thirty minutes later, David pulled onto the gravel driveway of Casey's cottage. Like Adam, David was familiar with the O'Grady place. *Small towns,* thought Casey and just shook her head.

As David helped her carefully exit the car, Rachel came running out of nowhere. Casey was nearly knocked off her feet but David held on tight. His arm was wrapped around her waist and he was strong. She didn't bend down to pet Rachel though.

"Rachel! Sit!" Adam commanded from the lane. "Hi Doc! What's going on here?" Adam asked as he sauntered over. Rachel was sitting obediently, tail wapping the ground, looking up at Casey.

"I see your training is coming along nicely." Casey smiled at Adam.

"Yes. Miracles do happen." Adam smiled back.

"So you two know each other?" David interjected.

"Not exactly. Rachel, this puppy, likes to come around." Casey said.

"What happened to you?" Adam asked.

"Oh just a minor collision with fate." Casey said. *Where did that come from? It sounds like I was supposed to meet David.*

"What I mean is, I nearly got mowed down by a motorcycle. Dr. Hawthorne saved me." Casey clarified.

"Oh, I've seen that guy buzzing around town. One of these days he's really going hurt someone. This is bad enough. Are you okay?" Adam asked.

"Yes, I'll be fine. I just need to take it easy for a few days. All good." She wasn't comfortable being the centre of attention, especially as an 'injured' person.

"Well, that's good. If you need anything, just give me a call okay?" Adam pulled a business card out of his jeans pocket. "I live four houses over. As you can see, I'm around several times a day, walking Rachel. So it's easy for me to drop around or pick up something for you."

"Thanks Adam. I may take you up on your offer. I'll see how it goes." *He has the most beautiful blue eyes I've ever seen.* She thought as she put his card in her pocket.

"Come on Rachel. Let's go, so Casey can get inside. It looks like we are about to get another downpour." Adam leashed Rachel up as the clouds overhead deepened in colour.

"See you Doc. Looks like you were in the right place, at the right time, as usual!" With that Adam and Rachel headed back down the lane.

"See you around Adam." David said as he guided Casey onto the porch. She dug out her key, with David's arm still holding her tight.

"What did he mean by that? Right place at right time?" Casey asked as she inserted the key and the door popped open.

"That's a long story for another day. Hey, this place looks good! It's been a while since I've been inside."

"Really? How do you know this place?" Casey was curious now.

"Oh listen, that's also a story for another day." He smiled an amused grin. "I'm really not trying to be mysterious, it's just that I want to bring your groceries in and get you settled before my shift at the hospital."

"Oh please, don't let me keep you. You've already gone far beyond what anyone would expect."

"It's fine. I have just enough time to unload the food and get going."

What a great guy! But she was also feeling ready to drop. David eased her onto a love seat and placed the comfy throw over her. He bent over the logs and proceeded to put a fire on, then turned on the lamps before he returned to the car to get the two grocery bags. *He sure seems right at home here. Maybe he is. Wonder why?* She put her head back and relaxed into the sofa while the heat from the fireplace began to warm her feet. *Enough for one day. I don't need to know his connection to this place. Not today, at least. I really am tired.* She thought as she closed her eyes.

Next thing she knew, David was touching her hand gently.

"Here's a glass of water and your pills as well as a cup of tea with a few biscuits. Before I go, do you need anything else?" He had a concerned look in his eyes as he gazed down at her. "I hate to leave you like this. Do you think you can manage?"

"Oh David, thank you. Sorry, I must have drifted off. Between jet lag and hospitals, I'm bagged. I can manage for now."

"Would you mind if I drop by after my shift to check on you? Or do you just want to sleep?"

Casey was touched. "I'm very tired, so yes I'll likely just crash."

"Sure. I would like to check in with you in the morning then. Would that be okay?" David looked into her eyes.

"I would like that. Thanks David." She smiled weakly at him. *Who could resist this guy?*

Chapter 14

Casey

asey slept deeply her second night at the cottage. In the morning her back was stiff and painful but she felt her sleep had been healing. She gingerly worked her way off the bed then managed to put on some comfortable baby blue yoga pants with a striped blue, pink & yellow tee shirt and matching hoody. Then because it was chilly in the cottage, she also threw on her thick yellow housecoat. "There, now I'm warm." She said out loud. Getting dressed had aggravated her back, so she decided to sit at the writing desk overlooking the garden, before she tackled eating or building a fire.

During the night each time she rolled over, the pain in her back woke her. As a result she had a lot of dark night thoughts coming up. Memories of leaving Robert and her resulting hospital stay. All the painful rehabilitation she had gone through. It was a rough night, yet towards morning her thoughts had been filled with the kindness of David and pictures of Adam's blue eyes and lazy smile. When she awoke she felt reasonably rested.

After she carefully sat on the desk chair, she eagerly looked outside. It was lush green everywhere. The singing birds looked like they were having their own celebration this morning. There must have been twenty of them, swooping down and soaring up again in circles around each other. She felt like she was eavesdropping on a private ritual. "This is amazing!" She breathed in a whisper. One of Casey's core beliefs was that Nature is God: all healing and all life giving. She was so happy to have this gift unfolding before her eyes.

The garden itself had a few cobblestone walkways through a cove of trees and shrubs. A little garden shed set over on the left side which looked like an inviting little house. *I cannot wait to explore this yard.*

She heard a car drive onto the gravel outside. A car door slammed. Footsteps on the porch, then a knock on the door. Casey slowly stood up, straightened her tender back and walked to the door. She looked out the glass window to the right of the door to see David standing there so she opened it.

"Good morning David!"

"Good morning yourself. How does your back feel this morning?" David entered the cottage as Casey stepped aside.

"I think I'm doing pretty well considering it could be much worse!" Casey quipped as she closed the door.

"Good. I see I'm just in time to light the fire and put on some water for tea or coffee. I brought us a few scones which we can have with the Havarti cheese in the fridge. Sound good?" David comfortably hung his jacket over one of the love seats and stood there looking at Casey. "I must say you look well rested and pretty this morning." David looked deep into her eyes.

Casey was a little taken aback at his directness although she kind of liked it. "That sounds about perfect David. Do you always spoil your patients like this?"

"Not a chance. The good news is, you are not my patient, so I am therefore free to spoil you. If you don't mind, that is." He smiled tentatively waiting for her reply, thinking he may have overstepped.

Casey laughed. "I definitely don't mind." She sensed his vulnerability and found it endearing.

"But first I want you to see this." Casey took his arm and walked him slowly over to the desk. She felt close to him again. "Look at all the birds! They are having a celebration or something!"

"They certainly seem to be. They may be putting on a show for the new person living here. Who knows?" He stayed close to Casey while they watched the birds. She was hyper aware of this muscular, blond athletic guy with the dark eyes standing close. She thought how easy it would be to turn into his arms, but didn't. *What is wrong with you girl? You are not ready!*

"How about if I get the kettle going while you make the fire? Then we can both sit down together."

"You're on." He handed her the bag of scones.

Fifteen minutes later, they were seated beside each other looking into the garden, sipping tea and enjoying fresh warm scones with cheese. After a few minutes of comment on the amazing garden and flock of birds outside, Casey had to ask: "So how is it that you know this property, if you don't mind me asking?"

David cleared his throat. "That is part of the whole gruesome long story I mentioned before. But this is not a day for gruesome stories. Agreed? You have enough to contend with here so simple rest and relaxation is what's called for. Tell you what. When you're well enough to go for a short hike, I will take you to one of our scenic spots and we can saunter and sit while I fill you in. Basically, it would simply be too much, too soon, right now. Trust me."

David looked into her eyes with such sincerity that Casey said "I won't argue with that logic. But now I will have to cap my imagination so I don't go on too many 'what if' tangents." She smiled at him. "Really it's okay. I am just glad you dropped in." *There, I said it.*

"I too, have an interesting story to tell, about my back injury. So you too, will have to wait. As you say, too much too soon!" She grinned teasingly at him.

"Ahha. Good return Sabrina! Do you watch tennis?" David changed topics masterfully and they kept the conversation casual.

Casey suddenly heard a commotion outside on the porch. It took about two seconds before she figured out it must be Rachel running onto her porch with Adam soon coming up the steps behind her. One bark confirmed it. That was Rachel all right.

David offered to go to the door.

"Hi there Doc!" Adam said as the door opened. "Sorry about interrupting. Rachel has decided that Casey is her new friend. Now every time we walk by the place she looks for Casey. How's the patient doing today?"

"See for yourself. Come on in." David said with little enthusiasm. Casey carefully turned to see Adam and sensed some tension between the two men.

"Good morning Adam! Please let Rachel come in too." Adam let Rachel go. She bounced over to Casey, jumped up on the love seat and snuggled close.

"This is the best medicine a girl could have." Casey so missed having a dog.

"I think I will get going now." David said.

This isn't awkward at all. I didn't orchestrate this so I will just relax and let it unfold. Casey was a great believer in life unfolding as it is meant to.

"Okay, thanks much David, for the goodies and your help." Casey glanced at the fireplace.

"Hey, I don't want to interrupt." Adam said.

"No, it's okay I should get going anyway." David replied as he grabbed the door handle. He turned back to Casey. "Take it easy. May I bring you dinner tonight? I'd like to check on you anyway."

"That would be great, if you aren't too busy?" Casey hesitated. She nearly invited Adam, but decided it might not be a good idea.

"No, I'm on days off starting tonight. See you later then." David stepped outside without another glance at Adam.

"Come on in Adam. Would you like a tea or scone?" Casey asked.

"No thanks. I think I will just take Rachel and carry on our walk." Adam said cheerfully while thinking, *I should have known David would move right in on her.*

"Oh. Okay. See you then. Bye Rachel!" And gave the squiggly pup a quick scratch as Adam picked her up off the love seat.

"Like I said, if you need anything just give me a ring."

"Thanks Adam." Casey smiled at him and realized she was a bit tired. *Must be the meds...or jet lag.*

After Adam left, Casey covered up with her throw and fell asleep within seconds.

Suddenly she awoke in a cold sweat. She had been dreaming or rather having a nightmare and she shuddered with the memory. In her dream, her car was barreling over a cliff - then she woke up. This was a recurring dream which she had been having since her altercation with Robert.

"I need to get outside." Casey said out loud. She carefully got up and opened the French door leading to the garden. As she stepped outside into the aromatic lush backyard, the fragrance of heather hit her. She glanced left to find a huge patch of it growing along the rock wall. *So lovely! Someone has obviously put in a lot of thought and care to design such a haven of beauty and tranquility. I must ask the owner for the background of this place when I email him.* Her eyes continued a sweep of the private space. Right beside the heather, were some huge vibrantly colored hydrangeas. The blue and purple flower heads were the size and shape of a large grapefruit. Casey had never seen a garden with so many of these gorgeous plants in one yard. Tucked in beside those plants was the shed which appeared to have a pathway going in towards the back wall. *I will find out what is behind there, another day.* On the right side of the shed were tall green leafy trees below which were a variety of colors with flowers, greenery and different colored grasses. One could say the ground cover was unattended but that was part of its appeal, to Casey, at least. Her eyes continued to the right where she saw a rock pathway into the trees, which wound in behind and then came out on the far right end of the garden. Half way down the right side there were more hydrangeas in pink as well as the purple and blue tones. *This yard is simply breathtaking. I am so lucky to have found this place.*

There was also a low wood deck across the width of the house where she could set up a writing space, weather permitting. *This is exactly what I need to calm my spirit and heal my body while I put Robert far behind me. Perhaps I will never return home!*

She went back into the cottage as she was feeling the chill but the fresh air had been rejuvenating. She had never understood why some people did not seem to take advantage of the outside world. *It's free, it's beautiful and right there to soothe one's soul.* She sighed contentedly, as she stoked the fire then made some lunch. Later, she sat at the desk looking out on the lush garden watching the birds, which were back again, doing their dance in the yard.

Casey began thinking about the two men who seem to have entered her world. *I'm definitely attracted to Adam but I know very little about him. I'm interested though. Probably due to his writing.* Casey felt that anyone who did serious writing must have a passion for it or why else would someone spend so many hours alone, struggling to say 'something'?

Now there is David. He seems almost too good to be true. My mother always told me: if something seems too good to be true, it most likely is. Oh well, it is fun having two attractive men around so I'll just go with the flow. Who woulda thunk it? But I need to get the memory of Robert and the guilt I feel, out of my mind and body.

In quiet moments, Casey was still saddened by the demise of her marriage and was trying to come to terms with the recent months before her fall and after. As she had not spoken to Robert she could only imagine how angry he was when he received the divorce papers while he was still in jail. She knew how much he would have obsessed over the need to talk to her meaning: try to talk her out of divorce. That, is likely why he still hadn't signed them yet. *It doesn't matter. I am moving on and he will have to also.*

Little did she know that as she had those very thoughts, Robert was on the plane getting closer to Ireland every hour, thinking about her too.

Chapter 15

Robert

I *probably shouldn't order another drink, but hey, who cares. No one is here to give me static. That's a good thing too.* " Robert often had a contradictory way of looking at the world. Casey had told him that he held any position which suited him in that moment even if it contradicted what he thought at an earlier time. *She can be such a bitch. Sometimes I wonder why I bother.*

As he drank his third Scotch, he was getting angry again thinking about Casey. Meanwhile, he was hatching the rest of his plan.

Before he left town, he and his buddy Andrew, went out for a drink at a local bar. Unfortunately Andrew 'lost' his wallet that night. Robert had decided in advance that he would get Andrew's wallet during their evening together. Robert figured that for this cause, his good buddy would want to help him out, getting Casey back. So all it really meant was that Andrew had the hassle of getting new ID and credit cards while Robert could move around under the radar when he arrived in Ireland. *I will make it up to Andrew later on, after Casey and I are solid again. I better not drink any more.* Robert told himself. They were about an hour from landing so he decided to lay back and catch a nap. *I need a clear head when I land. I'm glad that crying baby behind me finally shut up.* Robert closed his eyes.

Chapter 16

Casey

Casey sat down at the writing desk overlooking the garden, to email her landlord. She was thankful he left the Wifi code for her.

TO: Patrick, O'Grady
FROM: Casey Anderson

Dear Mr. O'Grady,

I am settled into your charming cottage now. I love it here!

The key was exactly where you said it would be.

I have a few questions:

1) Did a writer live here? The setup is so perfect for a writer, I had to ask.

2) Someone must have loved that garden as it was designed with such care. Any background you could share would be appreciated.

3) Everyone I have met so far, seem to know this house. How can that be? Is it just the small town thing or is there some big story behind this place?

That's all for now. I'm just curious, please feel free not to disclose if you prefer not to!

If I have any other questions I will email you.

Thank you again for everything.

Casey Anderson

SEND.

Casey had no idea where he lived or anything else about him at all. She was just glad she had finally sent him the email she had promised she would send, once she arrived.

She decided to catch a nap before David got there with dinner. Next thing she heard was a rap on the front door. It was only four o'clock so she was surprised David was early.

But she opened the door to a Pizza delivery guy, holding out a large pizza to her. She immediately thought David must have ordered it. But wasn't sure, so said "I didn't order a pizza."

The fellow had on large dark glasses, longish hair hanging out from under a ball cap. He spoke with an English accent and said "It's been paid for and here it is..." He practically shoved the box at her, turned around and returned to his car. *David must be on his way.* She took the pizza into the kitchen, turned the oven on low and placed the pizza on a rack.

I am feeling better and more mobile than this morning, so my rests have been good. I would love to go outside and explore this fabulous yard but I better not. I might miss David at the front door. That's another good reason to have a dog, they alert you! Casey smiled at her ongoing internal argument about getting or not getting, another dog, one day.

An hour later, Casey was still wondering what time David would show up. *Maybe he got caught up in an emergency and that's why he's late.* She was starting to get quite hungry when she heard a car pull onto the gravel, then the long awaited knock on the front door. She opened the door to see David holding a bag of groceries.

"Hi there. The pizza came well over an hour ago and I am hoping it didn't get dried out." Casey smiled at this gorgeous man.

"Pizza? That sounds perfect. We can eat this food another day then." David gave Casey a big grin.

"Didn't you order the pizza?"

"Sure didn't." David responded.

"That's odd. Over an hour ago, a guy showed up with a pizza, insisted it was ordered and paid for. So I took it, thinking you must have ordered it and were on your way over."

"Well that's strange all right. Do you have any other secret admirers around here?"

"None that I'm aware of." Casey frowned a little. She did not like mysterious events. Mainly because as a writer she could not let something go until she figured it out. She started to wrack her brain for who could have done this. Adam? No, he knew David was bringing dinner over. The only other possibility that went through her mind was her landlord. *That would be unexpected but he does know I'm here now and maybe he wanted to extend a gesture to welcome me. I cannot think of anyone else who would possibly do this.*

"Do you want me to call the pizza place and ask who ordered it?" David asked as he watched Casey thinking hard.

"Tell you what, you probably had a long day so why don't you just come on in and we can take a look at the pizza and decide if we want to eat it. I can always call them later or tomorrow. Wouldn't you just like to relax now?" Casey closed the door behind him and locked it.

"Honestly? Yes... I would love to sit down and share a meal with you. How are you doing now?"

"Much better David, I am happy to report." Casey headed into the kitchen with David following.

She put the pizza on the counter and they both looked at it. For the first time Casey realized it was the same toppings that she and Robert used to order. That sent a chill down her spine. Then she shook her head and told herself that many people likely order those toppings.

"Looks good to me! How about you?" David asked.

Casey told herself to get it together. She didn't want to ruin their time together right now, so she said "yes it looks delicious."

Ten minutes later they were seated at the wooden table sharing pizza and some red Chilean wine. Casey had not taken another pain pill, so decided the wine would do the trick in place of a pain med. She teasingly asked David if he would recommend wine versus Tylenol for her mild pain. He teased back and told her wine was perfect for mild pain. "Better than any medication. In fact, let's celebrate with a toast. You're feeling better, I'm not on call and can have a drink or two plus one of my very ill patients took a turn for the better today. Here's to us!"

"Cheers," Casey tried to join in with his jovial mood but a part of her was still feeling off about the pizza delivery. They chatted about their recent meeting and how each spent the day since. She wanted to keep it light as she was not ready to divulge her heavy past to David yet and she knew he wasn't ready to share his past either.

After the pizza disappeared completely and the bottle of red wine was empty, they went outside into the lush garden to check out the paths before dark. Ducking branches and stepping around overgrown shrubs was challenging yet fun for Casey but she soon realized David was not big on trekking through trees. He seemed worried about bugs especially spider webs. *Perhaps it's all that sterile training he's received. Or maybe he was toilet trained too early,* she smiled at her silly psychological reasoning. But the fresh oxygenated air surrounded by all that lush greenery did momentarily push aside her pizza concern.

Finally, she could tell David was getting bored outside so suggested they go inside.

"I'm sorry David, but I do feel like resting now."

David seemed a bit saddened to leave but he politely agreed she should rest. Casey felt awkward as she had the feeling he might have stayed on quite late but she really wanted him to go so she could check out that pizza order.

As soon as the door was locked Casey went back into the kitchen, found the pizza name and number and called it. The young man who answered had a thick Irish accent but Casey managed to understand him. She asked about a pizza delivered to her address around four pm that day. He put her on hold then returned to say they didn't have a delivery to her address that day. Casey then said "It was pepperoni, onions, feta cheese, mushrooms, olives with fresh uncooked tomatoes on top. Do you recall taking an order for that pizza?"

"Well, yes I do, only because of the uncooked tomatoes on top. We almost never get that request. We made that pizza up for a customer. Why are you asking?"

"I didn't order a pizza but that one was delivered to me. I'm just trying to figure out who paid for it so I can thank them. If I describe the fellow to you would that help?"

"Sure, I know almost everyone around here, so go ahead." He answered.

"Great! He was quite tall, maybe thirty something, longish blond hair, ball cap and jean jacket. Do you recall someone like that?"

"I sure do. He ordered the pizza, paid in cash and left. But he was definitely not a local. I've never seen him before. Does that help you?" The fellow was trying to be helpful which Casey really appreciated.

"Yes." She lied with her heart pounding. "That was helpful. Thank you very much."

Chapter 17

Robert

Robert was feeling pretty tickled with his deception. *Ha! I was two feet away from that bitch and she didn't even know it. The pizza delivery idea was ingenious,* he congratulated himself. He had deliberately ordered their favourite toppings as he wanted her to figure out that he was close by. *That will add a bit of mystery to my plan. She's likely torn between wanting to see me yet nervous. She should be nervous! That stint in jail was hardly fair. She'll have some grovelling to do to get back in my good books,* he sneered. He rubbed his aching head.

"This goddamn headache is worse than ever!" He cursed out loud.

Earlier, when he drove in from the airport, he followed Casey's address on his phone GPS, then chose a small motel near her place. He had already changed into his first disguise at the airport and was ready to put step one of his plan into motion. He had wanted to get a quick look at her and where she was staying.

Now, back in his motel room Robert began to prepare for his next move.

Chapter 18

Casey

asey is in a state of shock. She doesn't know what to do. *I think Robert has found me but how can I protect myself? What are my legal avenues? It is eight hours earlier in the U.S. but who should I call first?* Her anxiety is clouding her thinking.

She walked over to the front window to look out. Nothing suspicious. Just then Adam and Rachel were walking by her driveway. Adam saw her at the window and waved. "Adam!" Casey immediately wanted to talk to him. She went to the door and opened it. Rachel came racing over to her.

"Hi Adam, have you got a few minutes? I need a friend." Casey said unabashedly. Normally she would never be so bold but she had felt a connection with Adam and she really did need someone to talk to.

Adam looked pleased as he sauntered over. "I sure do! How are you doing?"

"I'm coming along but something has come up and I need an opinion. Come on in please."

Adam stepped inside while Rachel went running around the cottage in high gear.

"How about we let Rachel out back so she can exercise herself, is that okay with you?" Adam suggested.

"As long as it's fenced all around. Do you know if it is?" Casey asked.

"Yup, it is." Adam walked over and opened the door, Rachel took off.

"Oh to be so gleeful!" Casey sighed. " May I get you something to drink? Beer, wine, water, juice?"

"I wouldn't say no to a beer." Adam said. "But I can get it, you sit. What do you want to drink?"

"I'll have the same, thanks Adam."

Adam got their beers and settled down beside her on the love seat facing the garden. The outside light was on so they could watch Rachel running around sniffing all.

"You look like your back has improved a lot. But something has obviously got you tied up in knots." Adam looked into Casey's worried eyes.

"Yes. That would be an understated understatement." Casey smiled at him. She somehow knew they would share a love of words. "I will try to keep this brief but it is quite a story. Are you up for it?"

"Anytime. A good story will always be on my radar. Shoot." Adam smiled back and waited for her to continue.

Casey proceeded to tell him pretty much the Robert backstory. Berating herself as needed for her part in the initial departure from Robert. Always being sure to let Adam know that Robert had his faults but she did too. By the time she got to the pizza angle, Rachel had come back inside and was now cuddled on the love seat between the two of them.

After Casey finished the telling, she took a deep breath and scratched Rachel's ears, waiting for Adam to say something. She felt much better sharing her recent past with someone and was particularly glad it was Adam. He seemed to have space in his life. Whereas Dr David was so busy that Casey felt like he already had enough on his plate.

"Life is never simple is it Casey? First I want to tell you how sorry I am for what you have been through. No one deserves all that. Now to face the possibility that your Ex may be here is beyond disconcerting. So let's figure out your next step." Adam asked for her computer.

The first thing he did was a search under Roberts name. He found him in many different headings. He diligently went through about six of them confirming what Casey already knew about Robert. Then he found out about Robert's previous jail time and assault.

That one was a surprise to Casey and not a good one. The newspaper article was dated three years before he met Casey. He had been incarcerated for two years and seven months, which meant he had only been out of prison for less than six months when they met. Casey was even more distressed

"How can that be?" Casey said out loud. "He must have lied to me when he told me he had recently relocated from the Midwest and left his previous job with an Accounting firm there to start up his own business. Keep reading Adam."

They continued to read details of his crime: he had been charged with assaulting his wife; then she went missing.

"His wife? What? He told me he'd never been married! Oh my God! How can this be happening, Adam?"

Casey started shaking. Now she was really scared. Robert was a man she barely knew. Her imagination could take her places she did not want to go.

Adam leaned over and held her. Casey turned into his strong arms and began to cry. *This is all too much. I am in a foreign land, no close friends and now Robert might be here, stalking me?* She took some deep breaths and managed to calm herself.

"Look Casey, this situation is serious and we need to handle it accordingly. I'll help you and we will keep you safe, together. First things first, we need to get in touch with folks back in the states to confirm that he's not there. Then we'll get that Warrant in effect over here so that if he comes near you, he's under arrest. How does that sound? We take it one step at a time. Okay?"

Adam went on to remind Casey that this is a small community where the locals are very aware when a new person shows up. Everyone will notice. That could be the secret factor which Robert may not be aware of.

Casey agreed. She sat up and thanked Adam for being there.

"One thing for sure, you're not staying here alone. You may not be safe. Do you want to come and stay at my place, get a motel or I can stay here tonight?"

"It's late and we are here now, would you mind staying here tonight? One of these love seats is a hide-abed, I was told."

"No need, I can fall asleep anywhere. You just go get yourself settled and I will be out here." Adam stood up and gave Casey another hug as she got up.

"Good night Adam. See you in the morning."

"Good night Casey."

Chapter 19

Robert

obert was an early riser, always had been. Today he was particularly excited as he planned his next meeting with Casey. In case she had figured out he was close, he needed to act fast.

This morning he put on more of a local style to blend in. Jeans, white tee shirt and dark blue hoody. He had dyed his overgrown hair a red colour last night. Now he put on an Irish flat cap to finish off his look. He had been letting his hair get shaggy the past while as his normal look was quite groomed. *I need to look casual here, so I don't stand out.*

He had showered earlier as he was planning some up close and personal time with his wife today.

"I've gone far too long without any sex, so it's due." He said out loud as he put on the cologne Casey loved. *She is likely due too, finally.* Robert grinned.

"Yes today is the day, Casey my love. No excuses this time." Robert left the motel and walked out to his rental car with one thing on his mind: sex with Casey.

Chapter 20

Casey Plus

Early that morning, Casey got dressed and came out into the living room. She found Adam standing with his back to her, gazing out the front window. Rachel did not come bounding up so Casey knew she must be in the backyard. She joined Adam at the window.

"Oh good morning sleepyhead." He said as he gave her a hug.

He's one great hugger, thought Casey as she snuggled into his arms. She felt so safe. Like nothing could ever hurt her.

"Good morning yourself. Did you get any sleep?"

"Not a lot but that's okay, I got too much the night before. So I'm good. But now that you're awake lets get some coffee and make our plan."

"Yes, let's do exactly that." Casey smiled at him. *I am so grateful he is here. Everything will be okay.* In the light of day, the idea of Robert being close by did not seem so daunting.

They walked into the kitchen and a few minutes later, Rachel started barking in the backyard. Adam walked over to the garden window but he couldn't see anything that would make her bark.

Then a knock came at the front door. Adam told Casey to stay in the kitchen.

He opened the door and a fellow stood there with a paper in his hand. He asked Adam if he could tell him where this street might be. Guardedly, Adam took the paper and quickly glanced at it. Not quickly enough though. As soon as Adam glanced down, Robert pulled out a syringe and poked it into Adams neck. Adam slowly slid to the floor, just as Casey came around the corner and gasped.

"Adam! What happened?" Before Casey could kneel down to check Adam, the man at the door pushed Adam out of the way, stepped inside and closed the door.

"Hi wife!" Robert said. He was enjoying this. "I see you've already got my replacement. I don't think so sweetheart. You are still my wife and it's about time you acted like it."

"Robert? What the hell is going on? You cannot be near me. Get out now!" Casey was furious as she kneeled down to check Adam. Rachel was still barking in the yard.

"You always were funny Casey." Robert grinned at her. "Don't worry about your boyfriend, he'll wake up later today. Now c'mon it's time you and I got reacquainted." Robert roughly pulled Casey to her feet.

"Let's find the bedroom. We are overdue don't you think?"

"Not a chance in hell Robert! I said get out! Now, or I will call the cops!"

"Tell you what, love of my life, I won't hurt you as long as you shut up and cooperate. If not, well..." Robert pulled a short knife out of his pocket. Then a roll of electrical tape. "It's really your choice how this goes down. Cause it is going down."

"You bastard! Do you honestly think you'll get away with this?" Casey was getting frantic trying to figure out the best angle here. Robert really did appear to believe he was going to have sex with her. *Revolting,* she thought.

"Robert, be reasonable. Let's talk first." Casey tried to sound confident.

"Once again, you underestimate me, my love. Do you really think I'm that stupid?" Robert seemed suddenly enraged as if a switch had been turned on. He tightened his grip on Casey as he dragged her down the short hallway.

"Here we go." He said.

"No! Robert No!" Casey shouted.

Robert threw her on the bed then lunged forward to hold her down. He tore a strip of tape off the roll and put it over her mouth, from ear to ear.

"Now shut up Casey. Maybe once you shut up, that dog will too. If not, I'll shut him up!"

Casey looked at Robert with big eyes full of fear. Her back was already hurting again from landing hard on the bed. She realized he had her. There was little she could do now. He outweighed her by about 100 pounds. Also, she did not want him to hurt Rachel. In that instant she decided not to fight him anymore. She told herself this won't be any worse than all the times before when I didn't want to and went along.

But, in fact, this time was different. Robert was in a rage, as he unbuckled his jeans. He was thinking of his wife with that other guy; all the months he spent in jail and how Casey had gone half way across the world to get away from him. No way was she ever going to leave him for good. He sensed her change right away. That made him even madder. He wanted her to fight, then he could really give it to her. But suddenly, she was just laying there with her eyes closed, like she was praying or something.

"Open your eyes bitch. Don't want you to miss anything." She ignored him. He slapped her face, hard. Her eyes flew open.

"That's better. Now keep 'em that way!" Robert intended to hurt Casey and he did. She could not cry out but he could see it in her eyes. When the tears started he knew she was his again. At least that is what he told himself.

When he was done he left the tape on her mouth and added tape around her wrists, then her ankles. He did however, permit her to dress herself again, before he taped her wrists and ankles. After positioning her on the floor, he taped her bound wrists to the leg of the bed.

"Consider this our first date, so to speak, in Ireland, our new home." Robert leered at Casey who was sitting limply on the floor. "Once your boyfriend wakes up, I want you to tell him you are getting back with your husband and to stay away. Got that?" Casey didn't want anymore contact with him, so she nodded.

Just get out of here. Adam has to be okay, but I can't move. My back is killing me. Oh God, help us please, she prayed, trying to block Robert out. She had no more tears. It was more of a numbness setting in. Not feeling much of anything as Robert closed the bedroom door. She heard the front door close. He slammed it a few times. *He must have given up. It won't close tight without the key.* She heard his tires on the gravel. *Is he really gone? I have to check on Adam,* she vaguely thought. Wriggling her wrists was not working and only giving more pain as he had pulled hard on them, when he bound her to the bed.

Casey sat there on the floor, finally drifting off to sleep.

She awoke hearing David's voice. "Adam! Wake up! Adam! Where's Casey?"

Rachel was barking again in the background. Suddenly her bedroom door opened. David rushed forward.

"Casey! Are you okay? What the hell happened here? Was there a break in?" David was not his cool calm self now. He realized Casey couldn't speak, so first he gently pulled the tape off her mouth. Casey took a big breath and tried to speak, but no words came.

David undid the ankle tape quickly; then reached around her and tried to undo the wrist tape. He couldn't get it, so went to look for scissors. He asked Casey if she knew where to find them. She did not respond. He looked everywhere he could think of and finally found a pair in a kitchen drawer. He quickly cut the tape and Casey was freed.

"Casey can you tell me what happened?" David was being gentle now. He could see that Casey was in a fragile state. Casey just sat there not moving other than rubbing her wrists.

David went back out to check on Adam and call 911. Adam had a normal pulse so after the 911 call David went back to Casey.

"Can I help you to sit up Casey? Does anything hurt?" *It is much easier treating people you don't know. What happened here? Did Adam do something?*

Still no response from Casey. He went back to Adam and really shook him this time, calling his name. Finally Adam appeared to be waking up. He slowly lifted his head and saw David.

"What happened?" Adam slurred.

"That is what I want to know." David spoke more gruffly than he intended. "Are you okay Adam?"

"I think so. Where's Casey?" He asked as he tried to stand up. David helped him onto his feet. Adam carefully walked towards the bedroom.

"Casey's not in great shape Adam. But go see if you can get her talking."

Adam saw Casey sitting on the floor beside the foot of the bed. He knelt down next to her. He took her hand and gently said "Casey, it's me Adam."

Casey slowly raised her head and looked into his eyes. She started to tear up. Adam put his arm around her and she leaned into his chest. "You are going to be okay Casey. That son of a bitch will not hurt you again. That was your ex who came in right?" Adam asked. Casey nodded.

David stepped into the room and saw the embrace. Adam told David to call the cops. "This is a matter for the police David. We had a visit from Casey's ex husband this morning. He shot me up with something. God only knows what he did to Casey! Was she taped up?" He asked as he noticed the electrical tape on the ground near Casey.

"Yeah, let's discuss that later. I will call the police. The ambulance should be here any minute. Both of you need to be checked out. We need to find out exactly what happened here."

David called the police number. He simply said there had been an intruder and two people had been injured.

Adam held Casey quietly soothing her while she held on tight to him. Soon sirens were heard then a police car pulled into the driveway. David let them in and told them they could check out the scene but questioning would have to wait until both parties had been seen at the hospital. "The lady has been particularly traumatized." He told them. The police questioned David first. He gave this statement:

"I dropped over today after my shift at the hospital to check on Casey. She is recovering from a back injury. Right away I noticed that the front door was not closed tight. As I entered the cottage I saw Adam slumped on the floor. I tried to wake him but I got no response. I checked his pulse, which was normal. I found Casey behind a closed door in the bedroom tied to the bed leg with electrical tape. Her wrists, ankles and mouth were bound with tape. She was nearly catatonic. She would not speak or respond to me at all. I immediately called 911, then called the police shortly thereafter. I finally got Adam to wake up and he went in to sit with Casey. She seemed to respond to him somewhat. Then you arrived. Adam told me Casey's ex husband did this. That's all I know. Those two should be able to explain more later."

The police thanked him for his statement, just as the ambulance pulled up. Two medics came in, a woman and a man. After a few minutes quietly speaking to both Adam and Casey, they went back to get a stretcher. While the medics readied Casey for the stretcher Adam briefly checked on Rachel outside. She still had water and food from the night before so left her outside. Casey was carefully put on the stretcher. She immediately reached for Adam's hand when he came back over to her. They told Adam he could ride along in the back with Casey and off they went. David followed behind in his car.

Chapter 21

Robert

I *think everyone is overreacting a little bit.* He was parked around the corner and hiding in some bushes watching the activity at the cottage. *It will settle down soon, once they find out that she is fine.*

"It could have been a lot worse!" He muttered angrily.

Then he watched as Casey was carried out on a stretcher with that guy holding her hand. *How sickening. Casey always was a drama queen. That's okay, once they all clear out I will go back and do a little surveillance techno so I can watch Casey's comings and goings while I plan our next rendezvous. It's just a matter of time and she will come around and accept that I'm still her husband and the only guy who will ever love her properly. Other wimps would give into her whining, but she needs to know who the boss is. For better or worse, I'm not giving up. Not ever.* Robert was not a patient man so he decided to take off for now and come back in a few hours to scope out the house.

Chapter 22

Casey And Adam

*O*nce at the hospital Casey appeared to be feeling better. When she insisted that Adam get checked out too, he took that as a good sign and went along with her request, though thinking it was a waste of time.

They did a Rape kit on Casey and checked out her back injury. Her back was inflamed again, but no serious damage. More rest required though. Casey was starting to get angry again and muttered "thanks again Robert."

Will this nightmare, that is Robert, never end? She vacillated between anger and helplessness. She much preferred to feel angry but was so sorry that Adam had been caught in the middle. *I feel guilty now for asking him in to help me. But who knows what Robert might have done if he hadn't had to get out of there, knowing Adam would wake up? He couldn't have known Adam was there. Unless he had been watching the house and saw him come in. Perhaps that syringe, was meant for me. He intended to kidnap me! Stop Casey. Turn off your imagination now!*

Adam walked into her room. *He looks so good. He's my antidote for this nightmare.* Casey was relieved to see him.

"Adam!" Casey smiled the first smile since her ordeal. "Did you check out okay?"

"I sure did. They just said to drink plenty of fluids to flush the drug out of my system completely." He did not tell her that the same drug could have killed him at a higher dosage. The Doctor told him he was a very lucky guy.

"But how about you?" Adam asked.

"So far, so good. My back will just need more rest. Frustrating, but it's good news really. The rest will just take time. I should be fine, if I can ever get over this anger!" Casey wasn't joking.

"Do you feel ready to give the police your statement yet? I'm going to meet with them now and tell them what I know. I'll let you give the background story on Robert okay? That's your story to tell. Likewise, David was asking me about your Ex but I told him it's not my place to speak about it. Fair enough?"

"Thanks Adam. I really appreciate that and everything you're doing. I'm so sorry you got hurt." Casey had tears in her eyes as she looked into Adam eyes. He took her hand.

"Casey as far as I'm concerned you and I are in this together. I cannot explain it, it just is."

"I completely understand and I feel the same way." Casey said quietly.

Adam leaned over and gave Casey a warm hug. She impulsively gave him a quick kiss on the cheek.

"You talk to them first. Then I should be ready. Thanks Adam."

Chapter 23

Robert

Two hours later Robert returned to spy on the cottage. Soon after he watched the cops take off. *There won't be any evidence left behind at the scene anyway. I wore gloves, I'm not stupid! It's Casey's word against mine.* Then he snuck through the side trees and began his break in. He was good at opening locked doors and it wasn't long before he heard the click and it popped open.

Quickly entering the house he took a quick scope of the main room to pick out his surveillance location. "Yup, right in that upper corner. From there I can see the whole living room, front door and partly into the kitchen."

There was a tall cabinet on which he could attach his camera/recorder. He dragged a chair over, stood on it and went to work. Just by tilting it he could get a lot of scope and the best part was, it was virtually impossible to see from below. In ten minutes he was done. A quick test to make sure it was coming through on his phone. "Yup, there I am. The sound is working too." As he grinned into the camera.

Rachel was going crazy barking. *Its a good thing dogs can't talk,* Robert chuckled to himself. *Now I'm gonna get out of town, have a burger and beer somewhere. Reward myself for a job well done.* Robert was pretty pleased with himself, with little thought or concern for how Casey was doing. He wasn't happy about leaving the door unlocked but he couldn't find a key hanging up anywhere, so he had no choice. *I will just close it as snugly as I can and maybe no one will notice. Or they will just think someone forgot to lock it. No sweat.*

Chapter 24

Casey & Adam

At the hospital Adam wasn't very long giving his statement to the police, mainly because he had not been conscious while Robert was in the cottage.

"I opened the door to a man asking for help to find an address. As I took the paper he handed me, to read the address, he stuck a needle in my neck. That's all I recall until Dr. Hawthorne woke me."

The police asked for a description and all Adam could remember was red hair, cap and about 6 ft tall, average build. They thanked Adam and left to speak with Casey.

Casey was nervous in her hospital cubicle. It was a horrific story and she was dreading the interview. *But I know it is important if I want Robert found and charged. Which I do! As soon as possible, like now.*

Casey began her detailed account, then stopped and asked if the male officer could leave. They agreed and the female officer continued to listen, while Casey tried to hold her emotions in check. Although she was thankful that she had emotions again. It had been scary not feeling anything right after the rape. She had never experienced that before. But she had never been raped before either.

"I need to tell you that I am not on birth control. I'm concerned about getting pregnant."

"Let's take it one step at a time. Make sure you tell your doctor though. There are remedies they can give you now, to prevent pregnancy."

"I do not believe in abortion, so I don't think that's an option for me. But I will talk to the doctor, thank you for mentioning that though." Casey liked this kind officer.

She made sure they understood that so far, she had seen him in two disguises, neither which fit his actual look.

"I don't have a picture of him."

"Not a problem, we will get one from the Garda in Washington."

Finally she was finished. The officer asked her a few more questions then the male officer returned. He assured Casey they would contact the police department in Tacoma, Washington in the U.S., get the legal status on Robert and proceed from there. Once they confirmed the existing Restraining Order in place they would effect a Barring Order here, essentially the same thing in Ireland. That would give them a legal reason to pick him up for questioning and take it from there. By that time, the DNA results from the rape kit would be in and Robert could be apprehended until a court date was set.

After the police left, her doctor came in and Casey told her about the pregnancy concern. They discussed options and Casey found out that in Ireland, the 'Morning After Pill' is available over the counter and she can wait up to five days to decide.

But because Casey was against all unnecessary medication, as well as an anti abortion advocate, she would not consider such a pill, especially not even knowing if it was necessary.

"I respect your position. Do you want any pain medication? Are you up for anymore visitors tonight?" The doctor wanted to keep Casey in overnight and she had agreed as she was worn out and nervous about returning to the cottage.

"Yes, I could take a bit of medication. Not too strong though. Visitors? Who?" Casey asked.

"There are two men outside, Adam and Dr. David. Also, there will be a policeman stationed outside your room tonight. That should help you sleep better." The doctor waited while Casey thought for a moment.

"I would like to see Adam. Would you mind telling David I can see him tomorrow? But please be sure to tell him Thank You for finding us."

"Sure. He will understand. I'll also let him know you are doing as well as can be expected, if that's okay with you? I know he will ask how you are doing."

"Sure" Casey yawned.

Adam quietly came in after the doctor left Casey and signalled to him it was okay to step in to the room. Casey looked up and saw David looking in. She gave a little wave. He nodded back.

Adam pulled up a chair and took Casey's hand.

"Is there anything I can bring you from home Casey? How about some clothes?"

Casey was a bit embarrassed but she needed clothes to wear home tomorrow. She trusted Adam and felt very close to him after their shared trauma.

"That would be great Adam. Just grab whatever you see there. You should probably get home and get Rachel. Poor thing, she will be wondering what's going on. The door must have gotten locked so here are my keys." Casey reached into the drawer beside the bed where the officer had put them earlier.

"Okay, I will go now and let you get some rest." Adam gave her another hug. Casey held onto him. She was unaccustomed to feeling this vulnerable and she really didn't want him to leave at all. But she was exhausted. He must be too.

"Thanks again Adam for being here. Goodnight." Casey gave him another peck on the cheek. Adam kissed her on the forehead, smiled at her and left.

Casey turned out her light just in time for the nurse to return with a pill for her to take.

"Good timing." Casey said and took her pill then closed her eyes. It was then she got bombarded with ugly visions of the rape. She practiced deep breathing along with visualizing beautiful scenery. She had meditated for several years before she met Robert and found the practice still came in handy, from time to time. Finally, Casey drifted into a deep sleep.

Chapter 25

Adam & David

avid was still waiting outside in the hall when Adam stepped out of Casey's room.

"Hey Adam I figured you might need a ride."

"Oh good idea. I forgot I have no wheels here. Thanks a lot. I have to stop at Casey's place to get Rachel and pick up some clothes for Casey."

"Sure, no problem." Said David who was definitely getting the sense that Adam and Casey were getting closer since the ordeal today. He was a bit miffed but was not going to show it. Not if he could help it anyway. *How on earth could she choose Adam over me?*

When they pulled into Casey's driveway, both immediately noticed the door was not closed tight.

"Do you see that Adam? Think we should call the police first? He could be inside."

"Agreed. Do it." Said Adam. Rachel wasn't barking, so while David called the police Adam walked around the side of the house to check on the pup. Just in case, he grabbed a big stick laying beside the house which must have broken off the tree there. As he approached the rear fence, Rachel suddenly started barking.

He quietly said, "Rachel its me. Quiet! Sit!" Rachel listened to Adam and stopped barking. Adam saw her though the shrubs, sitting there with her tail thumping. Very excited but trying to behave herself. Adam took a dog treat out of his pocket and gave it to her through the fence.

"Good girl Rachel. Stay." Adam went back to David's car and got in.

"Dog okay? Police should be here any minute." David was abrupt now.

"Dog is good. She must have been sleeping when we pulled up. No sign of anyone back there."

The police arrived just then, two male officers who quietly told Adam and David to stay in their vehicle.

They pushed open the door and entered the cottage with guns drawn. After about five minutes or so, they waved the two men in. One of the officers had been on the original call and he knew the front door had been locked, as he was the officer who gave Casey her keys back, at the hospital.

"So I ask myself, what did this guy want to get inside for? It's usually one thing. To plant something. And that something is typically surveillance systems. Sure enough we found one." The officer said with a smirk.

"No kidding! This guy is the real deal! Trouble with a capital T!" Said Adam.

"You got that right. We are going to have to either watch Casey 24/7 till we catch this guy or she has to stay elsewhere for the time being. This is one sick bastard!"

"I'm sure glad Casey stayed at the hospital tonight." David said.

"He could be watching us right now. So let's get that thing out of here." The two officers set up a chair, climbed up and removed the camera carefully bagging it, to sweep for prints.

"Let's take another look around to make sure that's the only one." The officers checked all the rooms and found nothing else, while Adam grabbed a few items from Casey's room and found a bag to put them in.

"We're done here. Don't hang around too long it's not safe. We'll speak with Casey in the morning before she leaves the hospital."

"Thank you officers. I'll just get my dog from the yard and then we'll lock up." Adam shook both officer's hands.

David waved to them. He didn't care for the way Adam seemed to be taking over. He was used to being the one in charge.

Chapter 26

Casey & Adam

A dam walked into Casey's room at the hospital the next morning. "Good morning sleepyhead. How was your night?"

Casey was sitting up in bed looking at the breakfast on her tray. Adam discretely put the bag of clothes onto the bed.

"My night was decent considering everything. But I'm glad it's over. I am dying to get out of here. I don't think I can stomach this particular cuisine though."

Adam looked at the soggy scrambled eggs and dishwater-like coffee. "Don't blame you."

"How was your night Adam?" Casey looked into his eyes and saw concern there.

"Let's just say it was interesting. The police will be by today to see you before you are discharged."

"Why? Tell me, did they find Robert?"

"Not yet, I'm afraid. But they did find a surveillance camera recently installed in your living room. Your door was open when David drove me over there last night to get Rachel. So the cops came and now they need to speak with you again."

"Oh no! What's next?" Casey was shaken but trying to be strong. *Stay with the anger, not the tears,* she instructed herself.

"I can't go back to the cottage I'll be a sitting duck!"

"My thoughts exactly. So why don't you come stay at my place at the sea? I would bring you to my home, down the road from the cottage, except that Robert has seen both me and Rachel, so he could find you too easily. At my sea house, we can keep you safe. As long as you would feel comfortable with that."

Casey's head was spinning. All of this was too unreal.

"Adam that's so sweet of you but how could I possibly impose on your life that way?"

"How? Well, try this on: if the tables were reversed and I needed a place, I feel fairly certain you would step up and give me a hand. Am I wrong?" Adam smiled at Casey and continued.

"But the offer only stands if you are entirely comfortable with the idea. You can even get the cops to do a background check on me, if that will help. We don't know each other very well. Hell, maybe I should get a background check on you first, too!"

Now Casey grinned at that. *This man can sure make me feel better in a hurry, just by being here. He's good medicine for me right now.*

"Let me chew on all this for a bit okay Adam?" Casey reached for his hand. "And thank you for the clothes." She shyly looked at the bag he had placed on the bed.

A nurse popped her head into Casey's room to ask if the police could speak with her now. Casey agreed and asked Adam to put her tray back on the meal cart when he left.

The two officers from yesterday came in. The female officer began:

"We found a surveillance camera installed at your cottage. It's possible it was done in the past day or two. So probably after his intrusion, when the place was empty. This tells us that he is not worried about breaking any laws which makes him dangerous. We don't want you to return to the cottage until we have him in custody. Can you make arrangements?"

"I suppose I can. Would it be better if I just go home to the States?"

"Not really ma'am, he would just chase you there. How is it that he found you in Ireland anyway? Did you tell him or did someone else?" The senior male officer spoke up.

"That's a good question. I have been wondering that myself." Casey was trying to think how he could have found her.

"In that case, given his techno leanings I'm guessing he had a tracking device installed somewhere around you. Perhaps your cell phone, which we would like your permission to check out. We would need to take it for a few days while our IT Dept searches it. But meanwhile we should check out all your personal belongings before you go to wherever you are planning to stay. Otherwise, it's possible he will simply follow you there too." He glanced at his female partner.

"Okay, whatever you think officers." Casey's nervousness was getting replaced by anger.

"We will need your keys so we can go back and check out all your personal effects. Once everything is cleared, we will accompany you home to take what you need. Sound okay?"

"Adam has the house keys and he is right outside. Oh officers, could you do a background check on Adam for me. I'll pay for it. He offered to do one for me, as I may stay with him, but I don't know him very well."

The female officer grinned at Casey. "I happen to know Adam personally and I feel better knowing you will not be alone. We'll just get Adam to sign a release and will be happy to do that background check for you at no charge." The male police officer frowned at the officer but then shrugged.

The officers found Adam, got the keys and got him to E-sign a release for a background check, then they headed down the corridor talking.

"Hey boss, this poor gal comes all the way to Ireland for her dream holiday likely and this happens to her? We can afford to offer her a little Irish goodwill can't we?" Teased the female officer.

"Oh I guess so. You know me, always thinking about the bottom line. I would hate to have to lay you off!" He quipped. She punched his arm in jest.

Chapter 27

Robert

arly the next morning before he checked out of his motel, Robert discovered that his surveillance camera was no longer working. The last thing he saw, on camera, were four men standing around the living room talking. Then one of the police officers climbed up towards the corner of the tall cabinet and suddenly his screen went black.

He did have the pictures of both men who seemed to be around Casey. *That blond one was called doc, by that other guy, who was called Adam. That's the guy who opened the door when I visited Casey. Maybe I should have given him a bigger dose after all. He might be a nuisance I prefer not to deal with. I'm not sure about that doc guy. Is he really a doctor or is it just a nickname for some reason? A veterinarian... or a drug dealer?*

Robert went to the dingy motel office and checked out. He told the counter girl that he still had a few things left to pack up and would be gone in ten minutes. He returned to his room and changed into his next disguise.

"Change of plans dearest wife. No problem. They are looking for a guy now, who doesn't exist." Robert snickered to himself as he checked himself out in the mirror.

"This is the most fun I've had in ages." A few minutes later he left the motel dressed in a pair of tight fitting jeans, a beige knee length car coat, red turtle neck, gold dangling earrings, flat gold shoes and small black handbag. He shook his long brown hair wig as he adjusted his sunglasses. The red lipstick felt sticky on his lips. What women have to go through, he thought to himself. Robert headed back to Casey's cottage to watch and wait.

Chapter 28

Casey & Adam

Casey had just been cleared by her doctor to leave the hospital. Now she and Adam were waiting for the police to come back.

David stopped in to see Casey. While he was there, Adam stepped out to get coffee & bagels, for the three of them. Casey wasn't up to telling David the whole gruesome story, and he seemed to accept that, though he seemed a little distant. She wasn't sure exactly, but he definitely wasn't his usual friendly self. She was relieved when Adam got back to the room.

The police showed up and asked the two men to leave the room. After they left, the male officer began telling Casey what they had found in their search of her personal items.

"We know how Robert tracked you here to Ireland. He had a tracking device put into your brown tweed suitcase."

"What? That's insane!" cried Casey.

"That may well be. But the fact is we found it and believe there is nothing else in your belongings which he can use to track you. We have checked all the local motels, hotels and B&Bs in and around Dublin, nothing under his name. Of course, he likely is not using his real name. We would like to get you out of the cottage and to your temporary residence if you know where you are going."

"The background check on Adam has been completed and it's an all clear. Is that where you will be staying?" The female officer asked Casey.

"Yes. You can get the details from Adam. Can we go to the cottage so I can get my suitcases and prepare it for lockup?"

"We will escort the two of you now. Do not do anything other than pick up your belongings as we want you in and out quickly okay?" Said the senior officer.

Within the hour, Casey and Adam walked out the front door of the cottage, locked it and thanked both officers. The officers assured Casey that they would be doing regular drive by surveillance at Adam's house by the sea, plus they would provide a police escort out to the house now.

As Adam had already loaded Rachel's doggie goods and his own necessities into his trunk earlier that morning, they were set to go. Rachel was enthusiastic to see Casey in the car. "Come cuddle Rachel." Casey said as she snuggled with Rachel in the passenger seat.

The three of them headed towards the sea house with the police ghost car following them.

Chapter 29

Robert

Robert was getting impatient with all this waiting around, watching from behind shrubs, one property over. He watched as Casey and the others went into the cottage briefly then came out with Casey's suitcases in hand. He quickly tapped the GPS app on his phone only to discover the suitcase device had also been disabled.

"Score two for the pigs." Robert sneered. "That equipment isn't cheap, you are costing me Casey!" He hurried to his car around the corner a block away and returned in it so he could watch which direction they drove. He was a little surprised to see the police vehicle staying behind Casey's vehicle. *They won't be looking out for a woman driver.* He chuckled to himself. *Looks like they are heading out of town. Good, that will be easier to keep them in my sights especially with two vehicles. Thanks guys!*

"I should have been a detective." Robert muttered as he followed the two vehicles from behind a few cars.

Traffic was heavy as they drove out into the countryside, getting further from town. There were some acreages and country stores along the way but after a while, Robert started to wonder. *Is it possible they are leading me into a trap, out here in the middle of nowhere?* Fewer cars were around now but he was staying at least two vehicles behind and right now he was behind a large cattle or sheep truck which kept him quite hidden. *Settle down buddy, don't get paranoid. Just think about when you have Casey back, all to yourself.*

Abruptly, he saw the vehicle with Casey make a turn to the right. The police vehicle followed. He took a good look at the lay of the land as he kept driving. After five minutes or so, he turned right, into a side road and parked.

I have to remember what I saw. There was a large older house with a few out buildings. Those would make great hideaways. The driveway in was thick with trees and shrubs but I could still see the house from the road. Can't tell how close it is to the cliffs behind but it looks like a fair distance. Pretty fancy place. Robert frowned. *What is going on here? Are the cops putting her up? Is this her boyfriend's place? I need to find out how many people are there.*

He quickly turned back onto the highway and drove back past the property. Just as he did, he saw Adam carrying in Casey's suitcases from the car. *So she will be staying here.* He saw the police vehicle had already left. 'Perfect. Thanks again guys. You make my job so easy." He bragged out loud.

Chapter 30

Casey And Adam

Adam set Casey's suitcases down on the hardwood floor near the front door then he joined her in the huge living room which faced the sea. She was looking out and moved closer to Adam when he approached.

"This place is beautiful Adam. Is it yours?" Casey asked as Adam wrapped his arms around her from behind, as they both gazed outside.

"It is now. When my father died my mother insisted I take this over. That was five years ago now."

"I thought you said your parents lived in Seattle."

"Yes, they do. My mother and her new husband. He's a great guy and I tend to call them my parents now."

"Oh, I'm sorry about your father Adam. It's good your mother found someone." Casey paused and took a deep calming breath as she gazed at the seascape.

"You are one lucky man Adam. This setting is stunning!"

"I am a lucky man, that is for sure!" Adam gave Casey a squeeze.

"I am even more lucky to be here with you, Adam. I have no idea what I would have done without you. I can hardly recognize

Robert as the man I once thought I loved. How wrong can one person be? I have seen breakups bring out the worst in one or both parties. I am truly shocked at Robert's behaviour though." Casey was grappling with all that had happened and was doing her best to hold herself together.

"You should be safe here Casey. I'm glad we have each other too. It's great to have company for a change. I have security lights outside, so if anyone were to get near, we'll know it. I also have a few guns here. Would you like some target practice tomorrow? I'm serious." Adam was experiencing his own emotional ride, worrying about Casey.

"One step at a time Adam. Let me think about that. Right now I need to sit down and rest. Let's just hang out here and watch the sea." She grabbed Adam's hand.

"How about if I put on some music. Something quiet and calming?" Adam asked.

"Perfect" *Everything will be okay.* Casey kept telling herself, to stay calm.

"Then I'll rustle up a bite to eat. Are you hungry?"

"I could eat a little something, may I help?" Casey asked.

"Nope. Just rest easy okay?" Adam gave Casey his lazy grin.

Just looking at him smile makes me feel better.

"Rachel is having fun out there, chasing the birds who appear to be teasing her."

"Yes, they have their little games." Adam was setting sandwich fixings on the kitchen island.

For the next few hours the two of them watched the distant sea as Rachel ran around outside. They ate some lunch and talked easily then finally got around to talking about writing.

Casey told Adam briefly about her counselling background and how she had recently given that up to write full time.

"At least until I decide to go back for my Master's degree in Psychology, someday. Now I'm not so sure about that. I started writing self-help articles some years ago and have several published here and there. I'm tossing around a few book ideas, I just haven't settled on which one to focus on. So that's kinda my story."

"Good for you Casey! Do you have any idea how many people want to quit their day job to write but never get the courage? I guess it helps if you can afford to do it, but really, if that is the pull, more people should be brave enough to take the leap. I am so thankful I did. And I bet you will be too. Especially now that you have some serious connections." Adam smiled slyly at her.

"What do you mean, connections? I suppose you are a publisher." Casey teased back.

"Not at all, but I am a fairly successful author. Have you ever heard of John Atworthy?"

"Of course, who hasn't? So...? What are you saying?" Casey looked at Adam.

"Well, just between you and I, that is me. I write under that name. But few people know it. Whenever anyone asks me what I write, I don't lie exactly. I just say I'm working on a novel and would rather not discuss details. The next question is usually, have you been published and I just say, I'm ever hopeful. Normally, that takes care of any further questions. It's a bit awkward at times. Especially when certain people treat me like I'm a big loser. But my ego can take it." Adam chuckled.

Casey was speechless. She looked at Adam to see if he was joking. He seemed sincere.

"Well, what other fantastical secrets do you hold within, Sir Adam?" Casey teased him.

"I still have a few, for sure, but I bet you do too." He gave her a hug, then stood up and changed the subject. "Do you feel up to taking a stroll out to the sea?"

"Ummm,... I'm kinda feeling draggy but let's go anyway. It will be good for both of us and I will rest better after some fresh air."

Adam turned off the stereo and out they went. Rachel was ecstatic and jumped up from her sunny spot where she lay.

"Walk Rachel?" Adam hooked the leash onto her collar. "She gets so excited sometimes chasing a bird, that I can't take a chance she will go flying over the cliffs, once we leave the gated area." Adam explained to Casey.

The sea air was so fresh and exhilarating to Casey that she couldn't resist grabbing Adam's hand. Their eyes met.

"You don't mind do you?" Casey asked.

"Mind? I am guessing we are on the same wavelength my dear." With that Adam leaned down and kissed her forehead.

Casey liked the way he did that. *Not too much, too soon. Just right.* She smiled to herself.

They walked slowly, in comfortable silence until they got near the cliffs.

Casey had never seen anything like it. She was very moved at the beauty laid out before her. The whitecaps were crashing below on the rocks while mist sprayed high into the air as each wave exploded. The sky was a collage of grey and blue with white puffy clouds cascading across, carried by the wind. Casey could have stayed there forever, it was so inspiring. *If I were an artist, I would come out here everyday and draw or paint*, she thought.

Finally, she broke the silence.

"Adam, this place is magical. I really have no words, it's so beautiful here."

"I know. It never grows old either because it never looks the same. Every day, hell every hour, the light changes, the sky changes colour, the sea changes colours and tempo. It's endlessly fascinating. This house is where I escape to write usually. It's quieter out here than in town. So when I'm taking a break after a novel gets finished, I head into town to join the world, so to speak, hit the pub once in a while and catch up with friends. I have to say, your arrival in our fair town occurred the same day I had just come back into town. Your timing was perfect."

"I'm so glad! Otherwise, you would have been out here and I would never have met you. We're both so lucky!"

After a few more minutes, the wind was getting chilly so they turned around and went back to the house, arms linked together.

Chapter 31

Robert

After Robert found out where Casey and her 'boyfriend' were staying he went on a tour of their neighborhood. He drove up and down side roads to find the best access to the property without being seen. Finally, he picked out a dirt road which veered off the adjoining estate road and led to the rear grounds of the sea house.

"This will do, I think." Robert said out loud. He parked and started walking, after changing into running shoes and leaving the gold flats in his vehicle. *It's a good thing I'm in shape. But this wig is getting itchy. Better leave it on though, it goes with the earrings. Funny guy Robert.*

The ground was lumpy with lots of downed branches to step around as he tried to stay in the trees and out of sight as much as possible. *The last thing I need is to run into anyone. It's one thing to look like a lady, but a whole other thing to act and sound like one. I doubt I could pull that off.*

Finally Robert saw the back side of the estate including the two out buildings. He stayed in the trees while slowly walking forward. All of a sudden his left foot went down into a deep hole.

"What the hell?" Robert yelled without thinking. He went down on his right knee, then crashed to the ground twisting his left knee and ankle as his left foot got stuck in the hole.

"Ow! Ow!" He said as quietly as he could. "Great, just great! This is perfect!" He slowly, carefully pulled his left foot out of the hole. "That hurts man, really hurts." He winced.

Once he got his leg out he tried to lay down for a minute to feel what hurt the most. He couldn't but did gauge that his left ankle was by far the most painful, then his left knee hurt too. He determined his right knee was sore from landing on it, but not as painful as his left one.

"Okay guy, you've got one leg pretty much gimped. Whatcha gonna do now?" Robert looked around and found a long sturdy looking branch on the ground near him. He scooted closer to it on his backside, grabbed it and tried to stand up.

"Oh my god, that's hurts! Suck it up buddy. Move or die!" He did get up and very slowly made it back to his car. After painfully getting into the driver's seat he asked himself *how the hell am I gonna drive?*

He eventually figured out the only way, was to use his right foot for both the gas and brake pedal. Nothing else was possible.

"Good goddamn thing they use the wrong side of the road here. That really helps!" He said sarcastically. Before he left the area, he took off the scratchy wig and earrings, then rubbed off any lipstick still on.

Robert made his way back towards Dublin but stopped at a small motel with ground level entry which was close enough to Casey's new residence. In the car he changed into his jean jacket and managed to limp inside the motel office to check in. The counter girl was most helpful telling him the best delivery restaurants for food and even liquor delivery. He thanked her then slowly walked to the room, using the stick for support.

I guess my plans will have to wait little wifey. You'll pay for this too! "
Robert was mad again. In Robert's mind, this whole fiasco was
Casey's fault. He just wanted his wife back and feeling this much
pain, was not part of the plan. He ordered a chicken dinner, a case
of beer and settled in for the night.

Chapter 32

Casey And Adam

A dam showed Casey where her room was and she was impressed all over again.

"Adam this is irresistible! You may never get me outta here!" She joked as she gazed out to the sea.

"Hey, I'm not worried. You're welcome here as long as it takes. And don't you forget it!" Adam grinned at her while thinking, *I hope it takes forever. There is just something about this girl.*

Casey decided to try for a nap. Adam and Rachel left her alone behind her closed door. Then she heard the calming music come on again.

"Thank you for that Adam." She whispered.

As soon as she laid down, the memories of the violence with Robert, came flooding into her mind. Within that darkness lurked the fear that she could be pregnant.

Please God, do not let that happen. As soon as she married Robert and noticed certain character traits showing up, she began to doubt that he would make a good father. Robert had very little patience and was too quick to anger. Once Casey had decided she didn't want children with him, the unravelling of her marriage began. Her mother had always told her to look at a man and see if he would make a good father. If not, stay away! *I jumped far too quickly into that marriage. I should have taken a lot more time to get to know him. Who would ever think Robert was capable of such savagery?*

Her doctor told her they could test her blood in about seven days and Casey had the appointment booked.

I'll have to tell Adam. He deserves to know I'm not on birth control so anything is possible. I cannot even begin to process this whole baby idea.

After a half hour of restless tossing, it was clear to Casey that it was pointless to try and sleep. She got up and joined Adam and Rachel again, immediately feeling better in their company.

Chapter 33

Casey & Adam

*O*ne week later Casey and Adam were driving out of the hospital parking lot. Casey was visibly upset.

"I cannot believe it Adam! How can this be possible? I flew away from the U.S. and away from my soon to be ex-husband to start my new life. Now, here I am with a new wonderful man in my life, yet pregnant with a rapist's child! How is that possible? Life is so inexplicable at times. Why this? Why now?" Casey was getting herself worked up now. The shock which set in after her doctor told her, was now wearing off. Casey was told she might qualify for an abortion if she chose to go that route but it was also explained that abortion laws in Ireland are complicated and it could take some time, especially as the rapist was her husband. Although Casey didn't believe in abortions and had always told herself she would never have one, this situation was making her second guess that staunch belief. Unexpectedly, Casey had no idea what to do and had told her doctor that.

Now, in the car, Adam said nothing and let Casey vent.

Casey grabbed a Kleenex from her purse and wiped her eyes. "And to top it off, no one can find Robert! This is too much Adam!" Casey looked at Adam with tears streaming down her cheeks.

In the past week the Garda had confirmed several facts: there was no GPS set up on Casey's cell phone. They had confirmed the Restraining Order in the States; then activated a Barring Order, which is basically the same thing, in Ireland. Both facts were good news. No fingerprints were found on the Camera or at the cottage, not great news. This meant they could try to find Robert and hold him for violating the Barring Order but now they needed his DNA from the Rape kit to prove he was the rapist before they could charge him. Those results would be another week, at least. In the meantime he was probably running around looking for her. But the police were on the lookout for him too. Plus the locals near the cottage were also on the lookout for any strangers.

Casey felt ashamed of her outburst but really felt she was being pushed too far. *This is becoming exhausting and I am losing my grip. But it's also not fair to Adam*, she realized as she looked at him.

"I'm sorry Adam. This is hard on you too. What are you thinking?" Adam glanced at Casey while he drove. Over the past week they had gotten closer everyday. They discovered that they thoroughly enjoyed each other's company and both had mentioned that they were getting in deep.

"I think that we will take this one day at a time Casey. You and I have something pretty special and be damned if I am going to let this ruin it. Whatever you decide to do, I stand behind you." He reached over and squeezed her hand.

"Just so you know, this changes nothing in the way that I feel about you. Got that?" Adam said.

Casey looked at him thinking: *that is exactly what I needed to hear. This man somehow always manages to make everything seem okay. Is this what true love feels like?*

"Got it... I am so lucky to have met you Adam."

"The feeling is so mutual. Now, want to go have some fun?"

"Sure... that might be a good idea." Casey cautiously answered. *The way I feel right now, I cannot quite picture having fun, but I will give it a try.*

Adam turned off at a corner with the sign: N Lake Dr. They drove another few minutes while Rachel started to bark and jump around in the back seat of Adam's car.

"Obviously Rachel has been here before." Casey said. Her tears were dried and now she was curious.

"Yes, more than a few times." Adam pulled into a parking lot which was almost empty.

"Come on Rachel, let's go!" Now Rachel was even more excited and when the door opened she tore off towards the water.

"Rachel! Stay!" Called Adam. Rachel stopped in her tracks and waited for Adam and Casey. Adam quickly leashed her, so he could check out the shore before he let her go again. They walked up to the water's edge as Adam looked around and saw no other dogs. No dead fish on the shoreline either. Then he unleashed Rachel who went bounding into the lake with pure glee. She swam a little ways out then turned back to look at Adam, waiting for something. Adam pulled a bright orange ball out of his pocket and gave it a toss across the water. Rachel went after it, grabbed it in her mouth and swam furiously back to Adam. She dropped the ball at his feet, gave a big shake spraying both Adam and Casey. Casey was laughing by this time, right along with Adam.

"Here Casey, your turn now." As he handed her the wet slimy ball.

"Gee thanks!" Casey mocked. She took the ball, threw it and watched Rachel tear after it.

Adam was laughing as he told Rachel to just grab a handful of sand to clean her hands, after every throw.

"This IS fun Adam! What a great idea!"

Adam led Casey to a picnic table close to the water where Rachel could see them. He was glad to see a smile on her face again. He couldn't imagine how it might feel to have a baby growing inside you, especially under these nightmarish circumstances. All he knew was that he wanted to protect her.

"After we are done here, do you want to stop in at Flanagan's Pub near my town house. Have a beer and stew or soup?" Adam asked.

"Sure, are you hungry too? Let's do it." Casey was definitely feeling better. *Both Adam and Rachel are great company. I have to trust that God will guide me on this journey.*

An hour later they were sitting in a booth at Flanagan's, each with a cold beer in the noisy pub. Casey was pretty sure that drinking one beer wouldn't hurt the fetus. She vaguely recalled reading the latest story on that. I will do more research when we get home, she promised herself.

They both looked around for anyone who might resemble Robert in disguise. So far, no one suspicious.

"Adam, I don't know how you do it but you always manage to get me feeling like myself again. No matter what this old world throws at me!" Casey smiled weakly at him as she took another drink of her beer. "Life can be brutal at times, but I am finding out how important it is to have a good friend by your side to help you through the hard times. Honestly, most of my life I have been a 'survivor' meaning that I just depended on myself. That was one of many things Robert used to complain about, my independent streak. But now, I have you, my kind Sir, joining me amidst all this struggle and it feels good." Casey leaned over and gave him a quick kiss.

Adam liked how open Casey was with him. *She is easy to understand and trust, as I always know where I stand with her. Nice change. Nice lady,* he reflected.

"I'm glad that my presence is a positive for you Casey cause your presence in my life has definitely been the best thing that has happened to me in a long time. After my sister died, life was pretty grim for a while. She was my best friend really and missing her doesn't begin to describe it." Adam looked into his beer glass.

"Adam, I am so sorry to hear about that. What happened? If you want to talk about it."

"Sure, it's probably time. I thought David might have told you about it." Adam replied.

"Not a word." Casey waited.

"It was about five years ago that Brandy, who was twenty-one then, met David. The young resident doctor in his last year of training. They dated for nearly a year. She was madly in love with this older man, a doctor, of course. Every woman in town wanted Dr Dave." Adam said bitterly.

"What? Your sister dated David? Does that have something to do with the tension I always feel when you two are in the same room?" Casey was surprised.

"Yes, I guess you could say that. Anyway, it was Brandy's final year of University as well as David's. They were both pretty stressed but Brandy began having emotional problems and eventually was diagnosed with manic depression."

"Oh no, Adam. I know how challenging that disorder can be to live with and to treat."

"Exactly. That became part of the issue and David didn't have what it takes to hang in there. He broke up with Brandy. That same night, she took an overdose and was long passed before anyone found her." Adam started to tear up. He had not talked to anyone about his sister in years.

Casey moved her chair closer to Adam and put her arm through his.

"That is so sad Adam. I can understand why you don't talk about it much."

"She was really a fantastic person Casey. You two would have hit it off for sure. She was only a few months from Graduating with her teaching degree. I guess it was all just too much for her. Exams, losing David and her mental illness. It's hard to know what she went through. I guess part of me blames David and always will. Even though it was her choice and it may not be fair to blame him entirely but I can't seem to help it. Let's just say he's not my favourite person. I have to tell you, when I saw him bring you home from the hospital that first day, I was more than a little concerned. I was already looking forward to hopefully, getting to know you. Then, suddenly, there is Dr Dave hanging around."

"Ahhh, that explains a lot Adam. I get it now. I agree it's probably not fair to blame David completely, but then, we never know what goes on between a couple do we? I also understand why you would feel that way. That was your little sister and someone hurt her, when she needed them the most, perhaps. Relationships are so complicated."

Adam liked listening to Casey and always respected her point of view. He was glad he had finally told her about Brandy. *It was time to let Casey know where my melancholy comes from. If she's going to be around, it's going to show up.*

Casey was thinking back to the brief time she had gotten to know David and could only imagine how guilty he must have felt after Brandy died. *David seems to be such a caring person. This must be the story he was going to tell me someday.*

The waitress brought over their soup with Irish soda bread. Adam told Casey she was in for a treat and had probably never tasted anything like it, in the States.

"This is delicious. I could eat this forever!"

"I told you." Adam grinned at her. "I always save a bit to take to Rachel. She knows this place well and will be waiting for her share when we head back out to the car."

They finished their meal and headed back to the house at the sea. It was the first time they had left the estate since arriving there together a week ago. Both were thoughtful on the ride back to the sea house. Casey was pondering the new reality in her life that she was pregnant. Neither knew that their eventful week was about to take another turn.

Chapter 34

David

ver since Casey had left the hospital with Adam, David had not been sleeping well. *Just when I think I have finally found the girl of my dreams, what happens? Adam appears.*

David was again thinking that Casey would never choose that drifter over him, an established doctor. *I know that nearly every single nurse in this hospital would like to be my girl, but I'm pretty picky. Not to be egotistical, but I am a good catch after all.*

David had a background which he had never shared with anyone. His father had been a doctor too, in Washington state. But what no one knew, was that his father believed in and practised mercy killing, illegally, before he retired. He died shortly after retiring and did not live to see the state of Washington legalize Euthanasia in 2008. The only person he ever told his secret to, was David. At the time, David was still working on his science degree in the states and was not even sure he would go into Medicine. He had been shocked when his father confided in him and even considered reporting his Dad. But in the end he just couldn't do it. He would not hurt his mother or his father, in that way. Ultimately, he chose to turn a blind eye, in disgust.

That was then. Once David decided to go into Medicine and began to see first hand the reality of the suffering which many critically ill patients had to endure, his viewpoint shifted. He understood, finally, why his father did what he did.

More recently, there had been an increase in the number of sudden deaths in David's hospital. Besides ending the suffering of the terminally ill, this served the community in many ways, David told himself. For one thing, it opened up beds which helped the overall financial picture. It also relieved the hospital staff of the taxing burden of dealing with the dying which over time, can be very demoralizing. Finally, it aided the long suffering families so they could begin the grieving process sooner than otherwise and get on with their lives. In David's mind, it was a win win all around. *The fact that it happens to be illegal in Ireland, is beside the point. My duty, as a physician is to help my patients and by killing them mercifully, I am doing that in spades. If I get caught and am imprisoned, at least my life will have meant something.* David had considered returning to the States to practise Medicine and mercy killing legally, but he liked the simplicity, the storytelling and the culture of the Irish.

But right now, I am getting tired of waiting around to see if I can get something going with Casey again. I know we were just starting to get comfortable with each other before Robert assaulted her and knocked out Adam. Now that I know she is pregnant with her ex-husband's child, I could be there for her in ways that Adam surely can't. I just need to see her and spend time with her again. I'm sure I can win her over. It's my day off tomorrow, so I think I'll plan an outing and drive out to Adam's sea house and check in on her. David was not used to being turned down when it came to women.

The next day he arrived mid morning with a picnic planned, hopefully, for just the two of them. When he knocked on the front door, Adam came to the door, along with Rachel.

"Oh hi Adam. Is Casey around?" David asked.

"Ahh, sure. I'll get her for you. Come on in." Adam walked to the back patio, not a happy man. He returned with Casey.

"Hello David." Casey seemed surprised to see him and gave him a small smile.

David was relieved to see her looking much more alert than the last time he had seen her in the hospital.

"Well, you are looking much better I am happy to see." David was hoping Adam would take off and leave them alone.

"I thought you might be going stir crazy so I wondered if an outing on this beautiful day, might suit you. I brought food for a picnic if you are up to it. I thought we could take a drive out to the National Botanic Gardens. It's in Glasnevin County not too far out. Given your love of nature, I think you will enjoy it. Today is beautiful and the fresh air can't hurt." He put his dark brown eyes on Casey.

She was rather caught off guard and torn too. *I know how Adam will feel, yet David has gone to the trouble of planning this outing. I've enjoyed David's company and with his being a doctor, it might be worth discussing my pregnancy options with him.*

"Well, Adam was going to be heading into town soon anyway. I was planning to tag along, just for the company. But your offer sounds too good to turn down. Since arriving in Ireland I have barely gotten out to see much of anything. For obvious reasons, of course. Do you mind Adam?" Casey turned to see how Adam was taking all this.

"Of course not Casey. It's probably better than you sitting around in the car, for who knows how long, while I do my business in town." Adam seemed genuinely okay with it. But Adam was a good actor when he wanted to be. Like most of us.

"Okay then David, I'll go get changed. Then we can head out."

"Great." David breathed a sigh of relief.

As soon as Casey left the room and disappeared, Adam spoke to David.

"I want you to know that I recently told Casey what happened with my sister Brandy. We've been through a lot together now and I felt it was the right time to tell her. I wasn't sure if you had said anything but found out you hadn't."

"Never got the chance, Adam. No sweat. Thanks for the heads up anyway, I appreciate it."

"I didn't tell you for your sake. I told you so Casey wouldn't feel uncomfortable bringing it up. That's all. Take good care of her today. She's still building up her strength." Adam added. He suspected that David knew about Casey's pregnancy. If not, he soon would.

"Sure. No problem. I am a doctor." He said sarcastically. *This guy always has to goad me*, David thought as he turned to see Casey coming back down the hall towards them with Rachel following her.

"I'm ready. Sorry Rachel, you have to stay with Adam." Casey turned to Adam and gave him a smile.

"See you later Adam, good luck today."

"Thanks Casey."

David opened the door and the two of them left the house.

Chapter 35

Robert

obert was not having a good day, again. He was basically eating, drinking and stumbling around his motel room cursing Casey in a drunken stupor, much of the time. He was frustrated with his immobility and combined with his ongoing drinking, he had fallen several times. Overall the pain in his ankle was still quite bad but he could put a little weight on that foot now.

"I think I'm gonna take a cruise past the house and see if there's any action." Robert said out loud. It was early in the day, so he was still able to function somewhat.

"If I can't have you wifey, then no one will. That Adam guy has got to go, simple as that." Robert was getting darker in his thoughts about Casey and Adam.

His disguise today is longish hair, unruly dark beard, sunglasses and a cap pulled down. He limped out to his car and twenty minutes later he spotted the house from the highway. He sees Casey walking outside to a car, with the doc guy. *At least it looks like him. What the hell? How many guys is she stringing along now?*

Robert drives past the property, then thinks, *why not turn around and follow them? Maybe I can see what she is up to.*

He pulls the car over to the side of the highway, turns around and parks while waiting for their car to come onto the highway. He let a few cars pass then enters the traffic flow.

He follows them and a while later, Robert watches their car pull into the National Gardens turnoff, drive into the parking lot and park. Other cars are also pulling in, so Robert decided he would do the same. He parked at the far end of the lot, where he could watch them.

After they both got out of their car, the doc pulled a cooler out of the backseat.

"Aha..gonna have a cosy picnic?" Robert said out loud. He pondered what to do and realized he couldn't do much with his foot still hurting and decided to return to his motel.

At least I know you are still at that house and I can get ready to execute my plan, even if I can't act on it yet. This damn foot!

On his drive back to the motel, Robert finished off his step by step plan, in his mind, to finally get his wife back.

"This is great! It won't be much longer Casey, before you and I can begin our new life in Ireland, together." Robert went back into his room and poured himself a drink.

Chapter 36

Casey & David

As beautiful as Adam's house at the sea was, Casey had to admit it was great to be out in another scenic part of Ireland. The drive itself was spectacular with hills of lush green and purple heather mixing in with yellows creating an ongoing masterpiece.

"Now, this is stunning David. And we are not even at the Gardens yet!"

"Yes, the best is yet to come." David was hoping to have the whole day with Casey. *Maybe I can take her for dinner later too.*

After he stopped the car, David carried the cooler and they walked into the park where they found a bench in a pretty shaded spot surrounded by unusual plants and clusters of brightly coloured flowers. There was just enough of a breeze to make the warm temperatures comfortable.

"So pretty David. I can't wait to explore after we eat." Casey knew she wanted to talk to David about her pregnancy and about Brandy too but had not raised either subject on the drive.

They busied themselves by setting out the food and drinks. David had thought of everything, it seemed. He even had pickles and cucumbers, to go with the egg salad sandwiches. Cold, non alcoholic beer was the cue for Casey to mention her pregnancy.

"This looks perfect! Right down to the non-alcoholic beer." She gave him a quizzical look.

"Okay, okay...yes I know you just found out you are pregnant. But it was only out of concern for you, that I looked in your file. I hope you don't mind."

"No, not really. Actually, I was planning to discuss the whole situation with you anyway. Get your medical opinion, if that's okay?"

"For sure." David handed her a sandwich, then opened a beer for her.

"I'm still reeling from the shock I think. But the most surprising thing of all is that I find myself getting protective of 'it' now. So I'm starting to think that an abortion may be out of the question for me. I don't even believe in abortion, but until you've walked in those moccasins you never really know, do you? Yet, I go back and forth constantly, it seems. I find I'm even ambivalent about Robert. At one time, I very much cared for him and now I find his behaviour abhorrent. I know that people can show their worst sides when they are hit with divorce or separation, but I would never have predicted Robert would lose it, as he apparently has." Casey shivered.

"It's a big decision Casey. You will sort it out. Give yourself some time to adjust and think it through. Yes, a lot of men lose control when their women leave them. They can't handle it. Women too, as you know. It's similar to losing a partner to death, they cannot or will not accept it. They convince themselves they can get their partners back. Usually not. But then again, lots of couples do reunite over and over." David reached over and put his jacket around Casey's shoulders.

"Here, you're shivering."

"Thanks David. Well, I for one, have no intention of getting back with Robert. He's gone too far, baby or no baby!" Casey could feel her anger surging again. *I've got to get back to my Yoga. Keep myself calm.* She felt like crying, but refused to give in to it. David's compassion was getting to her.

"That sandwich was delicious, by the way. Thank you." Casey said to change the subject.

"Glad you liked it. Now, I wouldn't mind telling you my side of the story about Brandy."

"We are almost done eating so why don't we walk around a bit and you can go ahead." Casey thought a walk would make her feel better. *I always feel like I'm a patient when I'm with David. I guess I have been one!* She smiled to herself.

They packed up the cooler, left it on the bench and started following the trail which led into the Gardens.

"The air is so fragrant here. Too bad we can't take it home in a bottle." Casey mused out loud.

"I'm not sure how much Adam told you but the short version is this. Brandy and I had been in a relationship for about six months when it gradually became clear that she was suffering severe mood swings. It was almost as though being in a relationship was too much for her. At least, that was my take on it. I was honest with her and suggested as much. She didn't want to hear it and held on even tighter, as she entered therapy and started on the path of medication, after her diagnosis of manic depression. So I hung in for another four or five months, then just couldn't do it anymore. I was in my last year of residency and that is taxing, at the best of times. The drama with Brandy, was too much. I really felt I was doing the right thing by calling it off, finally. I tried to be a gentle as possible, but it didn't seem to matter. She lost it. She is an adult, so there was nothing I could do, really. I told her to call her therapist. She refused.

Her behaviour began to feel like manipulation, to keep me there. At the time I did not suspect suicidal behaviour at all, otherwise I would have called her therapist myself." David looked down at his hands.

"That must have been so hard to live with her death. I cannot imagine. Mental illness is very hard to deal with, precisely because it's not rational. All bets are off when trying to reason with a person who cannot reason. So I hope you don't blame yourself."

"I keep forgetting that your area is psychology. You are so right. I think I have come to forgive myself now. It would be great if Adam could too. But I think I just have to live with the fact that he will always blame me."

Casey did not want to get into that, so she said: "Well, thanks for telling me what happened David. I am glad you have gotten past it and are able to carry on. Life ain't always pretty, is it? That is exactly why I decided to take a break from counselling. It can wear you down after a while. Whereas writing is both freedom and fun!"

Casey was feeling much better and found the park to be a feast for her senses. *I love the colours, birds chirping, the scents of different flowers and the spray of water mists. This is an artist's playground, that's for sure.*

They kept their conversation light the rest of their time together. When David tried to prolong the day by inviting her to dinner, Casey declined. By the time they drove onto Adam's driveway, his car was there too. Casey was thankful he was there as she still didn't feel comfortable being alone. *Until they find Robert, I don't want to be alone. Especially now that I'm pregnant. That's still a startling notion which I can hardly believe. Maybe the tests are wrong. Stop it Casey, you need to get a grip and deal with your new reality.* She chastised herself.

Chapter 37

Robert

That very evening Robert was busy preparing for his next step.

"Yes, thank you Mr. Kelly. I'll see you at the house tomorrow morning around 9 o'clock and will try not to get lost!" Robert chuckled into the phone, being his most charming. Mr. Kelly was the owner of a house in the country for lease.

Robert calculated if he paid three months rent in advance, the owner would not bother to do a background check on him, especially as it involved contacting people in the US. *What name should I give him? Maybe I'll just make one up and see what happens.*

"I'm pretty good at convincing people to trust me, so I'm guessing it won't be an issue. Irish folk seem to have a picture of most Americans as wealthy, so he'll probably just take the money and leave it at that. If he's smart, anyway." Robert said out loud as he poured himself a celebratory drink.

"Tomorrow is the next concrete step of my plan to bring you home again wifey." Robert grinned.

My foot is starting to feel better so I just need to make sure I don't fall again. Might even take a nice walk beside Casey's place tomorrow and get some exercise, after I check out the rental property.

Chapter 38

Casey & Adam

When David pulled into Adam's driveway, returning from their afternoon at the Gardens, Casey wanted to run up and give Adam a hug. But she didn't, not with David standing there. Who, Casey noted, seemed to want to hang around. Although Casey had enjoyed her outing she was definitely in need of some quiet down time now. As it began to feel awkward inside the front door, Casey got impatient.

"I'm afraid I need to rest now David." *There, I said it. Enough already. I just want to be with Adam now...go! I must be getting tired and bitchy.*

"Oh, sure. Of course Casey. I have to get going anyway." David replied only to be accommodating. *The last thing I want to do is leave her with him. But what choice do I have? Maybe this is a lost cause.* David was discouraged now.

As Adam closed the front door, Casey leaned in to give him a big hug.

"There, alone at last!" She smiled at Adam then kissed him.

"I'm happy you're back too! I missed you, as crazy as that sounds." Adam no longer had to wonder how their day had been. *She is still my girl.* Which is what he had begun calling her, in his mind.

"Not so crazy my friend! I was eager to get home to see you too! So perhaps that makes us both a little crazy. Crazy in love!" *Oops! I didn't mean to say that.* Casey blushed.

"You are a brave one aren't you? Maybe crazy in love fits. Time will tell." Adam grinned and hugged her hard.

This is so easy. I can say anything to this guy and he doesn't panic or pressure me. He just might be perfect for me. You sure know how to deliver the good with the bad, don't you God?

"So how was the park?" Adam said while thinking, *I would have liked to be the one to take her there but there are still lots of amazing areas to show her. We will have lots of adventures together, I'm sure.*

Casey told him about their picnic lunch, the gorgeous gardens and their discussion about Brandy's suicide and finally, her pregnancy.

"David already knew I was pregnant so we briefly talked about that. He's easy to talk to about that kind of thing, being a doctor and all." Casey offered.

"I'm sure. It's still beautiful outside, so let's go sit at the back. I will get us some iced tea. We can watch Rachel tear around while we talk ok?"

A man who wants to talk, now there's a treat. Casey smiled inside.

"Sounds great Adam!" The afternoon outing had really helped Casey to feel like herself again. *I guess when life throws you curve balls you can either move and duck, or stand there and get hit. I'm going to move with the flow on this curveball.*

As they both settled down outside overlooking the azure blue seascape, Casey sighed contentedly.

"So how are you feeling now Casey, about the pregnancy?"

"I am still getting used to the idea, but it seems to be settling into my being. I find that I am feeling soft towards it. I doubt that an abortion is on the horizon." Casey looked into Adam's eyes.

"What do you think about that Adam? Have I shocked you?"

Adam laughed nervously.

"I think that whatever you do, I'm good with it. You have not shocked me. Rather I have lots of questions. Like where would you want it to be born, where do you want to raise the child, and how will this impact us, you and I?"

Now Casey laughed nervously.

"Whoa! Hold on! Can we agree to take this one step at a time, please?" Now they were both laughing...until Adam leaned over and planted a fierce kiss on her lips.

"Hmmm, what was that for?" Casey asked smiling.

"Just to let you know I'm in, step by step, for however long this takes to figure out." Adam said. *I am in this thing deep. Hope I don't get hurt.*

"Good to know Adam. Seriously, I'm so happy with you. Even with everything going on, I am happier than I have been, in quite some time. And you, mister, are no small part of that!" Casey grabbed his hand.

"Well, that settles it then..." Adam said.

"What...settles what?"

"I'm officially smitten and not afraid to say so!" Adam said.

"Well...me too! So no need to worry." Casey could feel her happiness pour into her new being growing within. She started to tear up. Adam noticed.

"What's going on Casey?" He gently asked.

"Oh, silly me. It must be hormones. I'm just so happy Adam. I almost feel guilty for feeling so good." Casey wiped both her cheeks.

"Hey, you deserve it. We both do." As he leaned over and kissed her.

Chapter 39

Robert

Robert found the rental house in the countryside, about twenty minutes from Dublin. *Close enough to run into town but far enough out, to be away from people. Nicely isolated, no close neighbours. Perfect for our rendezvous. If she doesn't come willingly, I'll have to keep her here until she is willing.*

An elderly Mr. Kelly was waiting for him and seemed to be taking a good hard look at him, Robert thought as he walked up to greet the older man. He had decided to call himself Bob Sloan and introduced himself according. They looked around outside the house first, then walked inside. *Its not the Taj Mahal but it's comfortable enough.*

They discussed terms and Mr. Kelly was about to pull out an application when Robert brought out a wad of cash and started counting out bills.

"Will three months advance payment be enough to get us started?" Robert asked with his most winning smile. He had told Mr. Kelly he was an accountant. When you tell people you're an accountant they tend to assume you are an organized, by-the-book sort and that can open doors, Robert had discovered over the years.

"Ah, well..." Mr. Kelly coughed uncertainly. "I think that will do nicely sir. I'm a pretty good read on people and once your wife arrives, I'm sure you two will settle in nicely. You can fill this application out, then I will have your contact information."

"Would you mind if I take it and mail it back to you? As it turns out, I'm in a wee hurry this morning. Also, I need to get a local cell number." Robert watched for the older man's reaction.

"Of course, that shouldn't be a problem. As long as I have your name and know where to find you, which I do." He chuckled. "Here are the keys. Will you be moving in right away?"

"If I get time, yes I plan to move in later today. My wife should be arriving by the end of the week. Can't wait for her to see it!" At least, that's the truth, Robert said to himself.

Chapter 40

Robert

With the rental house keys in his pocket, Robert started driving towards the sea house where Casey was staying. *My ankle is much better so I should be able to walk in and take a good look around.*

Robert had brought the stick to use for support walking through the trees between the two properties and planned to scout out approximately how far it was from the edge of the trees to the cliffs overlooking the sea. He had an idea in mind for his next and final visit.

As soon as he parked and got out of his car, he heard what sounded like a gunshot. "What the hell was that?" He muttered. It didn't sound like it was near him, so he kept slowly walking inside the tree line. Then he spotted a red jacket through the trees, it was Casey. She held a handgun while Adam stood close to her. Robert couldn't hear what they were saying but it looked like Adam was instructing Casey.

If I wasn't seeing this with my own eyes, I would never believe it. Casey shooting at a target? Who does that bastard think he is? Robert was infuriated. He walked further into the trees where he could watch the two of them. Casey and Adam were both laughing. That was the final straw for Robert. *I was planning to wait a few more days, but I want Casey with me now, I've had enough of that guy hanging around her!"*

He walked to the edge of the trees and could see how far away the cliffs were, not far. *That's good. A gun was not in my plans, but if I can draw that Adam guy away from Casey, we are golden. You are about to meet your maker, pal.*

He staggered out towards the cliffs, in the open now, where he could easily be seen. Yelling nonsense and walking like a drunkard, he kept an eye on the treed area where Casey and Adam were.

Sure enough, Adam came running out to see who was on his property. *He probably told his girlfriend to stay back, so he could protect her,* Robert sneered then noticed Adam did not have a gun. *Okay you son of a bitch, it's showtime!*

Robert kept weaving all over, edging towards the cliffs, while waving his arms and the walking stick, in the air. Adam got closer and called to him.

"Hey mister, what are you doing out here? You've got to go!"

Robert ignored Adam and kept heading closer to the cliffs. Adam reached him and grabbed his arm. Robert shook him off and kept going. *Just a few more feet and you are toast buddy!* Adam followed and grabbed him again. This time Robert grabbed him back. Then he heard Casey scream.

"Adam! Stop! It's Robert! Stop!" Casey was coming out of the trees now.

"Stay there Casey! Don't come here!" Adam was pumped now.

Robert took advantage of the distraction with Casey, to pull Adam towards the cliff. But he wanted to make it look like an accident, if he could. He wrestled Adam to the ground so neither of them would be clearly seen by Casey. Adam was fighting back now. They wrestled closer to the cliff. Robert decided this was the moment. He got a good grip on Adam, yanked Adam's one hand off his own shoulder, then gave Adam a strong kick towards the edge of the cliff. *I don't plan to go with you pal!*

Adam fell over the edge. Casey screamed. Robert immediately stood up and tried to look as though he was dumbfounded. He looked down the cliff side and there was Adam splayed out on a rock cliff only about eight feet below. *Goddammit! He should be way down on the rocks.*

When Robert turned back to see Casey, he saw the gun pointed at him. *Whoa, this is crazy. She wouldn't dare.* Then he nearly laughed out loud but decided not to rattle her any more than she already was. *Stay calm and reason with her,* he told himself.

"Casey, it was an accident! I tried to talk to him but he just wanted to fight. I'm sorry, it wasn't supposed to happen like this. I just wanted to see you and talk to you""

"Like hell, Robert. I have called the police and an ambulance. Your days of freedom are finally over." Casey said in a steely voice, gun steady. *Can I really do this?*

Robert couldn't help himself now, he did laugh.

"Casey, you could never, ever shoot me. Let's be honest. Come on now, give me the gun. You and I can have our second chance now. I have a house rented for us. We can go there now, if you will just see reason." He started moving towards her.

"You are a piece of work Robert. The only place you are going is jail. Do not take another step!" Casey was shaking inside but knew she had to act tough. All she wanted to do was run to the cliff to see what happened to Adam.

A distant siren could be heard. Robert was startled. *The cops! Too quick! I can't get Casey away in time! If I hurry, I can get outta the area before the cops get here!* Panicking, Robert turned and limped away as quickly as he could, heading for his car hidden behind the trees.

"Robert!" Casey screamed. "Do not move or I will shoot!" They both knew she wouldn't. At least, Robert hoped she wouldn't. Casey didn't think she would.

But she did, she pulled the trigger. *Oh my God, did I really do that?*

Chapter 41

David

Meanwhile, David does not realize his world is about to change. He is working in Emergency at the hospital, trying not to think about Casey. *Boy, I must have it bad. I cannot get that girl out of my head.*

The next thing he knew, an ambulance arrived with an injured man who had gone over some cliffs. David was called to take the patient. As the drivers told him the details of the patient's condition, David suddenly realized it was Adam. Then Casey appeared with red eyes and tear stains on her cheeks.

"Casey, what happened?" David rushed over to her.

"Just take care of Adam! He can't die David!" She was shaking.

"Okay, I will. But nurse, please take care of this woman too. She may be in shock and she is pregnant." He said quietly to a nurse close by.

"Yes, Doctor." She told Casey to take a chair where they could check her vitals. Casey didn't argue. She wanted the best for her baby. She tried to watch what they were doing with Adam.

Chapter 42

Robert

As Robert ran in the direction of his car, he heard the gunshot. He kept moving. *It missed me, I think. She did it! She pulled the goddamn trigger! That bitch!*

He knew his car was tucked away and could not be seen. He got into it and drove back between the two sea front homes. As he turned onto the highway, he could not see the flashing lights, but he could hear the sirens. *That's good, if I can't see them, they can't see me.*

He decided to go back the way he came. As far as they knew, he was just one of many passing vehicles. When he saw the flashing lights, he just stayed in the flow of traffic until an ambulance and police vehicle both went rushing by.

"That was a close call! Now I need to come up with another goddamn plan." He said out loud as he rubbed his aching leg.

"And I need a drink!" He drove to his motel and checked out. Then stopped at a grocery store to pick up some supplies and drinks, limping with each step.

Soon, he arrived at the rental house and settled in for the night. Or so he thought.

Chapter 43

Adam, Casey & David

David could tell that Adam was not doing well and his vitals confirmed that. But the team was determined to do all they could for him. As Adam was rushed up to emergency surgery, David walked down the hall to find Casey.

"Casey, he's injured pretty badly. He may have severed his spinal cord when he fell, but we cannot tell the extent of the damage until we get in there." David was going to assist the surgeons.

"Will he live?" Casey asked as she drank the water the nurse had given her, to hydrate her while in shock.

"At this point we are going to do everything we can to make that happen. Are you doing okay?"

"I will be. I just need to know Adam will live."

"Hang in there. I have to get going now." David turned to go.

"Good luck in there." She was struggling to hold it together.

Casey went to find out if the hospital had a chapel where she could go pray. It did and she made her way there. When she last saw Adam, he looked more dead than alive. She felt like her world was falling apart. *Can God possibly be so cruel as to take away the one thing that is starting to make me feel alive again? All of this is my fault! Adam was trying to protect me and now he may die. I wish that bullet had hit Robert! Oh God, forgive me but I cannot bear to lose the man I am falling in love with. He's such a decent, honourable man who would make a wonderful father.*

"Please God, keep him safe. Watch over him, I'm begging you." Casey had always prayed, as long as she could remember, but this was more focused than her usual prayers. She stayed in the chapel for a long time, not wanting to leave the peace which seemed to envelope her there. Not wanting to quit asking God to watch over Adam. Men and women quietly came and went as Casey kept her head bowed.

Finally, Casey left the chapel and went back to the waiting area. She knew the surgery could take a long time and it did.

Five hours later, David and the head surgeon came over to Casey. The doctor introduced himself and told her how the operation had gone.

"He made it through the surgery, so that is favourable. He is on his way to intensive care soon and will be there for awhile until his vitals are stable. We have completed the spinal repair and spleen repair. He lost a lot of blood but he's had two pints of blood now and looks better. There appears to be a possibility that he may never walk again and could be a paraplegic, if he makes it. Which we are hopeful he will. So now we need to pray and hope for the best. He will receive the best of care, but sometimes, that simply isn't enough. Are you close to him?"

"Yes, I am." Casey was barely able to speak as she tried to process all that the doctor had told her.

"Then I suggest you stay close and talk to him. Your presence may help this young man come back to us." The doctor turned to David, nodded and left.

"Oh my God David! Is Adam really that bad?" Casey looked at David helplessly.

"I'm afraid so Casey. He's has been very badly injured but you must never give up hope. We will know more in a day or two." David said.

"May I see him now?" Casey asked.

"He's still coming out of the anesthetic but I can take you to the Intensive Care waiting room and you can sit in there until they give you the go ahead."

"Okay." Casey gave David a forlorn sigh.

"Now that he's out of surgery, the police will want to speak with you. I asked them earlier to wait for a bit. But as it's late now, they may not come back until tomorrow. Meanwhile, they've been on the hunt for Robert since I briefly told them what you told me earlier."

"I can't even think about that right now." Casey was exhausted.

David led her to the waiting area outside the big double doors leading into Intensive Care. There were a couple of oversized comfy high backed chairs and Casey took one of them. David had grabbed a blanket and pillow from the linen room on the way there.

"Here, take these and get comfortable. Get some rest if you're able. Do you want a hot tea or juice? You can help yourself later too, as there should be a few things to eat in the patient kitchen around the corner." He pointed down the hall.

"Not right now thanks. Maybe later."

"I will be here for a few hours yet Casey, so just ask the nurses to page me, if you need anything ok? You need to take care of yourself too, you know."

"You're right. Maybe I should have a little something to eat and drink now, while I wait." Casey said.

David took her to the kitchen and showed her where to get hot water for tea and a small yogurt. He was glad to see her eat something. He really wanted to give her a hug but felt it would be inappropriate and he left.

Casey found her way back to the waiting area and wrapped herself in the blanket. Next thing she knew, she heard wheels rolling past her and woke up just in time to catch a very bloated Adam on a gurney going into the ICU. It barely looked like him. David showed up right after and explained that she would have to wait a little longer as they had to get him hooked up to all the monitors. Then she could go in.

"Why is he so bloated David?"

"It was a long surgery and they had to give him lots of fluids. That will level out in the next while. Try to prepare yourself, as he doesn't look very good. His colour should improve soon though. They had to give him quite a bit of blood. It's always difficult for family to see their loved ones in Intensive Care, hooked up to so many machines."

All Casey could do now was wait and try to have faith that he would be okay. Earlier she had called Adam's friend, Bonnie to ask her to go to Adam's house and pickup Rachel. Rachel had gone there once before, so Bonnie said it was no problem. So now, Casey took a minute to call Bonnie and let her know that Adam was out of surgery but still not out of the woods yet.

"I will keep you posted though." Casey said as she started to cry, again.

"You take good care Lassie. God will provide."

An hour or so later, a nurse came to Casey and told her she could come in and sit with Adam. Casey walked into the darkened area lit up mainly by bright monitors beeping away. *It's a good thing I can't see him really well. He definitely doesn't look good. Oh my God, if I didn't know better, I would guess he is dead. His colour is so grey, he's so still and the machines are breathing for him, looking like they are the only things keeping him alive.* Casey pulled a chair near the bed. *Poor Adam. I don't know if I can bear to see him like this.*

She took a deep breath, said a little prayer and took Adam's hand. She leaned over him and kissed his forehead, as tears streamed down her cheeks.

"Adam, it's me Casey. I'm here with you. You are going to be okay. Please rest and let your body heal. I love you." The words surprised Casey when they slipped out. But her heart was so full of love for Adam now, she couldn't help herself. She knew they had both been feeling it, but neither had declared their love.

"If you can hear me, squeeze my hand." There was nothing.

Casey sat down and began her vigil. She dozed on and off, slowly getting used to all the beeps and odd noises around her.

A nurse came over and woke her. It was morning already.

"There is an officer outside waiting to speak with you Miss."

Casey stood up and stretched then walked outside of the unit and the female officer was waiting. They found a quiet place to talk.

"This guy is sure creating a lot of havoc isn't he? I have some news. The DNA results are back and it is confirmed he is the rapist. So now, we have an all out search going on and most important, his picture will be all over the news on TV. We have a much better chance of catching him now. For your safety, we have an officer posted here at the hospital. Whenever you leave, an officer will accompany you, until we get Robert. Usually the public is very good at helping out at this point. We are fortunate that his picture from the states is relatively recent. That will help."

"That is good news Officer Delaney. You have been very supportive and I really appreciate it." Casey liked this woman. *Perhaps in another time and place, we could have been friends,* Casey thought in passing.

They went over the details of Robert showing up at the cliffs and the fight which ensued. Casey told everything, including the fact that she had taken a shot at him. The reliving of that scene got Casey shaking again, but she took some deep breaths and told herself to stay calm, for the baby's sake. Then she walked back to Adam's bedside, exhausted.

Chapter 44

Mr. Kelly, Landlord

Mr. Kelly was pretty sure the guy on TV wanted for rape, was the same fellow who had just rented out his house. He stewed about it briefly, then decided it was the right thing to do. He called the Garda and reported that he wasn't positive, but his new tenant looked very much like the wanted rapist on TV. He gave them the particulars and the lady officer said they would check it out right away.

"Please keep me informed. I need to know if this fellow will still be my tenant or not." Mr Kelly was not used to any drama in his quiet retired life.

"We will sir. As soon as we finish our investigation."

Chapter 45

Robert

obert was sleeping on the sofa when he heard tires on the gravel outside his front door. *It must be that landlord checking on something. I hope this guy won't be a problem,* he thought as he sluggishly walked to the window to look outside. All he could see was a dark blue car. Then heard a knock on his door. He couldn't see who it was, so he called out.

"Who is it?"

"We need some help. Please open the door." One officer called back.

What's going on? I don't have time for this BS.

"I'm not dressed. You will have to find help elsewhere." Robert is ticked.

"I don't think so. We are the Gardai, open up Mr. Paterson."

Oh oh, how do they know my name? How the hell did they find me? Think, Robert think! Robert started to panic. Just when he thought he would never get caught, here he was. Caught! He looked around and thought he might try to make a run for it, out the back door. *Nah, they are probably outside there too. My head is killing me and I can't think straight!*

"Hold on for a minute. I think you've got the wrong guy officers. I will just get dressed."

Robert quietly went into the bedroom, sat on the bed and thought about his options. He shook his head. *How did they figure out where I am? The point is genius...they've got you!* Robert argued with himself as he rubbed his throbbing head.

Okay, what is the best move now? The smart move? I think I need to surrender. I will admit all except pushing Adam over the cliff. I'll just say it was an accident and no one can prove otherwise. It will be Casey's word against mine and she wasn't exactly close enough to see. That Adam guy may be dead, but even if not and he says I kicked him over, I'll say it was not intended. I can beat this.

Robert went to the front door, opened it and raised his arms above his head in surrender. Then he collapsed.

Chapter 46

Casey

*L*ater that day, while sitting with Adam, Casey had another visit from Officer Delaney who told her that Robert was in custody and he had confessed to all, though still insisting Adam's fall, was an accident. The officer told Casey not to worry about that.

"The facts will come out over time as we investigate. But it appears that Robert was planning to kidnap you and take you to a country house which he had just leased. His landlord told us Robert's wife was supposed to arrive in a few days. We are so fortunate the landlord was on the ball and called us. Otherwise who knows what might have happened. Once again, the public came through for us."

Casey shivered to think what could have happened.

"Robert has an assigned lawyer and will be undergoing medical and psychiatric treatment. He appears to have an ongoing headache which they will check out. We want to speak with Adam as soon as he's up to it. You are now free to come and go, without any police escort. I'll keep you updated. Hang in there Casey." The officer left.

Casey slumped back into her chair. She was so relieved to know that finally, Robert was no longer a threat to them. But the rage she felt towards Robert shocked her. *I feel like I could literally kill him! He has taken away the only important thing in my world. Robert, you don't deserve to live.*

How can he possibly be the man I married? He must be a master manipulator who can be his most charming self, as long as all, goes his way. Of course, me being a counsellor, I missed all that! He totally duped me. Married before too, which means we probably aren't even legally married. Which could be one good thing, at least.

Casey had met many women and men too, who had felt completely blindsided by their partners. *Until it happens to you, you can't truly understand how betrayed and demoralizing it feels. My first marriage ended mutually. After one year together we both knew it could never last forever. He hated sex and I hated him!* She used to joke. *Now, enter husband #2 and of course, he is a near sex addict. I'm not exactly the poster child for success...Stop it Casey! All this negativity is pointless. We all make mistakes. That is how we learn and grow. Pick yourself up and carry on: that is the true meaning of success, never give up. Not easy though.*

She took Adam's hand again. "That goes for you too Adam. We must never give up."

Casey was good at self-counsel sometimes, but the rape, her exhaustion, her pregnancy and now Adam's injury, had nearly driven her to her breaking point. *I must get a grip! I have a life growing inside of me. My back is acting up again too. Please God, take this hatred out of me.*

Casey left Adam's side to go back to the chapel and pray. When she did, she finally began to feel calmer. *I wish I could take a long nap and have this nightmare be gone when I wake up. I understand 'denial' much better now. They say the brain will deny that which it cannot deal with. I get it. Feeling* a little calmer, her optimism sneaked in and she couldn't wait to tell Adam that Robert was locked up.

Over the next few days Casey got into a routine of spending most of the day at Adam's bedside and returning to the sea house each evening so she could bring Rachel back home for overnights plus get some much needed sleep.

Early on day three, Adam finally squeezed her hand in response to her request and later the same day, he woke up. He recognized Casey, though he was still groggy. Casey ran out to tell the nurses.

"Hurry, he's awake!" The doctor came in and asked her to step out while he examined Adam. Casey was pacing up and down the hallway when David came by. She told him both bits of good news; about Adam waking up first, then about Robert being in custody and confessing. David impulsively gave her a quick hug. Casey was a little surprised, *but he is a friend, after all.* She told herself.

David went in to see how it was going with Adam's checkup. Minutes later he returned, frowning.

"It's always difficult to give bad news Casey." He began. "Adam.."

Casey cut him off.

"Is he going to live David?" Casey asked frantically.

"It's looking better now Casey. I'm sorry to have scared you. However, both legs have no feeling or movement right now. There was extensive nerve damage, which they repaired but the doctor isn't certain if Adam will ever get back the use of his legs. I'm so sorry."

Casey was feeling like she might faint. She grabbed onto David who led her to a chair. At a loss for words, she kept picturing Adam outside playing with Rachel, standing in the kitchen cooking for her, the two of them walking out towards the sea together. *How is Adam going to take this?* David was silent as he watched her.

"How is Adam taking the news, David?" She looked into his eyes.

"Not well, I'm afraid. That's normal though. It takes a while for patients to get over the denial and come to acceptance, then deal with it."

"Thanks for being honest with me. I'm going to the Chapel for a few minutes." Casey stood up.

"May I tag along? Would you mind?" David asked.

"That's fine." Casey seemed detached and in her own world.

Casey walked up to the front row of seats, sat and bowed her head. David stayed further back, sat down and waited. He was not a praying man but he respected those who did. Even envied them a little.

It wasn't long before Casey stood up and walked back towards him. She gave him a hint of a smile.

"I want to see Adam now. Thanks for joining me."

When they got to the ICU, David left and Casey entered the ICU. Adam had his head turned away from her. She walked around to the far side of his bed and pulled up a chair so she was at eye level with him. His eyes were closed so she took his hand.

"Adam, it's me, Casey." She quietly spoke.

Adam kept his eyes closed. Casey thought he must be asleep so she just sat there, holding his hand, thinking and wondering what would happen now. She wanted desperately to believe that Adam would, in fact, be okay and walk again. But David hadn't mentioned that possibility. *Surely there is always hope, isn't there? It doesn't matter anyway. I love this man and I'm pretty sure he loves me too. So even if he has to live in a wheelchair, he's still Adam, the man I am in love with.*

"Please leave Casey." Adam spoke very distinctly.

"Adam, I want to be here with you. Can we talk about what the doctors told you?"

"Not now Casey. I need you to leave. You can stay at the sea house as long as you want. That will be good for Rachel. But I cannot see you right now."

"But Adam. You shouldn't be alone now. I can help you through this." Casey was getting scared now.

"That's exactly what I don't want. Your pity. Please go." Adam closed his eyes and turned his head away from her.

Casey, as a trained counsellor, knew that she should respect Adam's wishes and leave. It was very hard to do but she stood up to go.

Then she leaned over Adam, kissed his forehead and whispered, "I love you Adam Murphy. Don't you forget that!" Shaking with tears, she turned and forced herself to walk away from the man she had fallen in love with. *Damn you Robert!*

Chapter 47

David

avid was trying to focus on each patient who needed his attention but it wasn't easy. There were two issues needling him. He was torn about Casey's situation and trying to decide how best to handle it. *This is my chance and I don't want to blow it. Why am I so good at my work but so lousy at relationships?* This wasn't the first time he had asked himself that question. *Sure I feel bad for Adam, he doesn't deserve what happened. But Casey also doesn't deserve to be saddled with a paraplegic partner. I will be sure to remind Adam of that fact. If he cares for her at all, he'll get it.*

The other factor distracting David was his most recent mercy killing. The family members were upset that their daughter had died so suddenly. They were making noise and wanted an autopsy done. David now regretted deciding to step in on the poor girls' behalf. She was only thirty nine but had ALS and everyone knew it was going to be downhill from now on. Her prognosis, however was further complicated by her epilepsy. Every time he watched as her brain shorted out with another seizure, the urge to put an end to her suffering grew until he finally acted. It was the day of his outing with Casey. After leaving her with Adam he was so frustrated that he went back to the hospital and inserted the syringe which put that poor woman out of her misery. He needed the feel good endorphins which were released each time he 'helped a patient die' and ended their suffering. *But I know the hospital cannot support my decision and in this particular case, I see that the family wouldn't either. I thought they would be relieved. Perhaps I overstepped on this one.*

In spite of his busy day, he found himself hatching an idea which might suit both he and Casey and get him away from an investigation. The more he thought about it the more he liked it.

If I can get close to Casey again, we could return to the States together. She could have the baby there, we'd be far away from both Adam and Robert plus I could legally pursue Euthanasia. Well, more or less legally, anyway. That will get me far away from scrutiny here in Ireland. Casey might like the idea of going home, putting all this behind her, with her Doctor fiancé by her side. Who wouldn't want to marry a doctor?

David's mother had always told him growing up, that if he became a doctor, he could pretty much have any woman he wanted. He had found that to be quite true. *It just so happens that Casey, is the woman I want. I will find a way to get her. My odds have greatly improved now that Adam is at a huge disadvantage. Sorry about that Adam, but may the best man win.*

David went to find his next patient.

Chapter 48

Casey

When Casey arrived at the sea house, after picking up Rachel from Bonnie's place, she felt lost. Her joy with Adam's awakening had been short lived. His shutting her out was not easy to take.

The beautiful life I have been picturing with Adam is no longer possible. Adam is a changed man now. The question is, will he be changed for the better or for the worse? After watching Robert change so drastically, I am kind of wary. But I am not ready to give up, yet. Adam needs me now, more than ever and we need him too. She put her hands on her belly.

I just need to give him time to adjust to his changed life. Oh God, why did this have to happen to Adam? Such a deserving, decent man? Casey felt the tears coming again. *I need to adjust too, we both do.*

Casey's cell phone rang startling her. It showed Unknown Caller.

"Hello?"

"Casey?" A burly Irish accent asked.

"Yes, speaking."

"Casey me dear. Dis is the landlord callin' yer." The older man spoke with a strong Irish brogue.

"Oh, hello Mr. O'Grady. Is everything okay?"

"Aye. Ah've been 'earin' yer troubles miss. Are ye fine now?"

"Things have been difficult and are still up in the air. I am undecided if I will move back into the cottage just yet. But I intend to honour my agreement with you, don't worry."

"Now don't ye fret lassie. Oi jes wanted to make sure yer gran'."

Casey smiled. "That's very kind of you. I'm hopeful things will work out okay."

"I know yer Adam lass and oi wish 'imself well. If yer be needin' a mucker, call me gran'?"

"Pardon? A mucker?" Casey was confused.

He chuckled. "A friend, miss. Ye can call me an we can visit."

"Oh thank you Mr. O'Grady, I just may do that." Casey started to tear up hearing the kindness in his voice. *I really do need a friend right now.*

"Aye. Then I be waitin' for yer call. Take care nigh."

Casey said goodbye and felt warmed by her landlord's call. The Irish are something else, she thought. It really seems to be all about relationships, as opposed to the almighty dollar, like in the states. She did wonder how much he had heard via the locals.

Rachel had been trying to get Casey's attention while she was on the phone.

"Okay, okay little one. Let's go outside!" Casey was grateful for Rachel. Her enthusiastic energy could give anyone a lift. *I would love to be able to take her in to see Adam. I'm sure they wouldn't allow it though.*

She let Rachel tear around the fenced yard, then leashed her and they walked out to the cliffs. Memories of Robert and Adam wrestling on the ground near the edge of the cliff, came flooding back. Casey let them. She knew she had to face her fears and not let them haunt her. *Bring them on! I am going to be strong now, for Adam and this little one inside me.* She taunted herself, feeling the anger surge up. *Too bad that bullet missed you Robert! Forgive me God. I will work at forgiving Robert but I'm not even close to that yet.*

As she watched the surging sea crash on the rocks below, amidst her anger she felt stronger and grateful. *I am thankful Adam is alive. Thank you God, for that.*

Chapter 49

Adam

Adam was moved into a private room later that day. He was still hooked up to a heart monitor along with an oxygen mask, as needed, but he was doing well enough, breathing on his own. The doctors were more confident that he was capable of holding his own now.

Like breathing even matters, thought a very depressed Adam. *I would just as soon die than be forced to live in a wheelchair for the rest of my so-called life.* He tried not to think about Casey. *The pity in her eyes is more than I can deal with. I cannot handle her pain and mine too. That son of a bitch David will be all over this. He will move right in on Casey and there is nothing I can do, but sit back and watch. I have zilch to offer her now, that's for sure. Probably can't even have sex again. Kill me now.*

Adam was in as dark a place, as he had ever been. David had dropped around but Adam told him to leave. The only person so far, he allowed to stay, was the physiotherapist and that was only because she would not take no for an answer. In fact, she got downright aggressive with him. *Obviously, this is not her first rodeo,* he told himself, with a near smile at her combativeness. Her name was Cynthia and she was short, strong and feisty. Not to mention, cute.

That makes it even harder, Adam thought when she showed up the first time. *How humiliating is this, to be impotent and disabled in front of this looker?* Cynthia made it clear very quickly, that she would not buy into his 'poor me' attitude.

"You best be countin' yer lucky stars Adam! From what I heard, ye could be dead at the bottom of some cliff. So what if twenty percent of yer body isn't in great shape, today. The rest of ye is fine from what I can tell and ye better not be takin' that for granted. We are going to work those nerves and perhaps ye will be walkin' again in no time. Have faith dammit! Yer Doctor explained how your back injury was 'incomplete'. So that means there is a chance you can get those nerves workin' agin and we're not gonna give up!"

Cynthia assisted Adam with a few exercises in the bed, on day 1 of physio. She told him as soon as his incision is nearly healed, he will go down to the physio pool and that's when the real work will begin.

Adam was exhausted when she left, but he felt a tad better, he admitted grudgingly.

Chapter 50

Casey & Adam

When Casey arrived at the hospital, after lunch the next day, Adam had a physiotherapist with him. Nervous but determined she waited outside his room. That morning she had taken a picture of Rachel, then stopped at a shop and had a photo created which she then framed. It was tempting to include herself in the photo, but decided to see how Adam's mood was first.

While she sat waiting, David walked by and sat down with her.

"How are you managing Casey?"

"I'm hanging in there. Not easy, but hey, who ever promised life would be easy?" Casey tried to be flippant so that David's kindness wouldn't set her off crying again.

"Exactly. I tried to check in on Adam yesterday, but he wanted no visitors. I hope you have better luck today."

"That's what I'm hoping too." Just then the blond physiotherapist left Adam's room. She said hello to David on her way past the two of them.

"Think, I should risk it?" Casey smiled nervously at David.

"Maybe wait a bit, he is likely tired out after physio. I am on a break, why don't we go to the cafeteria and get a bite or a drink? Unless you're in a hurry?"

"Not in a hurry. In fact, a little energy booster might be in order. A courage donut or something like that. Do they sell those?" Casey smiled at David. She was determined to rise above this nightmare situation. It could be much worse and I'm going to be strong for Adam and this baby, she told herself.

A half hour later Casey entered Adam's room. He appeared to be resting or sleeping but he opened his eyes as she approached the bed. Casey said nothing but gave him a small smile as she put the framed photo of Rachel on his tray.

Adam did smile when he saw the photo.

"Well, aren't you the smart one? Bringing me something irresistible. How can I kick you out now?"

Casey was relieved that he seemed more together than yesterday.

"That was precisely my plan Adam. Besides Rachel misses you too. I wish I could sneak her in here. She is fine, by the way." Casey figured Rachel was the safest topic.

"She best get used to it, then." Adam sounded bitter again. "You too Casey. I have been doing a lot of thinking the past day or so. We need to be honest with each other. I have no future to offer you now. It's that simple. So I don't want you running back and forth to the hospital trying to cheer me up. There's no point. You have a life and you need to live it. I'll sort my so-called life out from here. You are welcome to stay at the sea house and take care of Rachel if you don't mind. It's the perfect place to write, so you may as well get on with your original plan. Just forget about me okay? It's best for both of us Casey."

Casey looked at Adam. That speech seemed very rehearsed to her. Likely it was, she told herself. It couldn't have been easy for him to push her away, but he seemed determined to do so.

She turned away and looked out his window, which overlooked a gorgeous green garden of trees, shrubs and cheerful wild flowers. She took a deep breath and said a silent prayer to keep from tearing up. I must be strong now, she told herself. What does Adam need the most from me right now? Understanding, she answered her own question. Another deep breath and Casey turned back to Adam.

"Adam...while you were out of it, I came to know that I have fallen in love with you. It is the very last thing I would have imagined, a few months ago. That would be fact number one. Fact number two, you want to push me away because you feel you will be a burden in my life. I completely understand why you feel that way, although I do not view you as a burden, because I love you. So where does that leave us?"

"Nowhere. It's simple, love or no, I can't allow your life to reduce down to the level of my new reality. Period."

Casey could feel herself losing this battle of wills.

"Well, who ever said the road to true love runs smoothly?" She attempted a smile. He did not smile back.

"Seriously, I'll respect your wishes. But don't expect me to drop off the face of the earth. I will take you up on your offer and stay at the sea house with Rachel. Remember you were my first friend in Ireland. Surely we can still be friends. I too, could use a friend right now. I have some decisions to make. Like where I want this baby to be born." Silence from Adam.

Finally he said: "Good, you have decided to keep it then?" In spite of himself, he did look happy for her Casey thought.

"Okay, we can still be friends but that is all." Adam continued. "By the way, the Garda came around and told me they have Robert in custody. I'm glad you are safe now. I gave them my statement, but my memory is fuzzy from the moment he and I both hit the ground. They told me it may come back. What did you see?"

"I couldn't see a lot after you both dropped down on the ground. It was so scary Adam! Once I recognized Robert though, I yelled for you to stop. When you didn't, I came forward. Suddenly you two were on the ground, near the cliffs. You went over. Then I pointed the gun at Robert and told him to stay put. I had already called the Garda. Robert came towards me and tried to get the gun. But when he heard the siren, he turned and ran past the trees and disappeared. I took a shot at him, but missed. When I looked over the cliffs, there you were. Thankfully, you had not fallen all the way down to the rocks in the sea. You landed on a jut out, not too far down. Then the Garda and ambulance arrived." Casey searched Adam's face.

"Thank God you and the baby are okay Casey." Adam's tone had softened some.

Yes, and it seems you do still care, Casey was thinking. That made her feel better. *He's not made of steel as he is trying to portray.*

"Yes, we are okay. The police told me Robert rented a house out in the country which he planned to take me to and hold me there. Basically kidnap me. It's beyond belief."

"Oh no, no. That's a nightmare to even contemplate!" Adam looked away.

"I know Adam. We are both very lucky. You could easily have been killed."

"So my physiotherapist keeps telling me." Adam gave a half smile. "I'm tired now Casey."

"Okay, I'm out of here. Take good care." Casey feigned casual calm. Being a counsellor for several years, she was practiced at that. She was planning how to be Adam's very best friend from now on. *We will be fine. We have to be.*

Chapter 51

David

After his shift was over, David dropped in to visit Adam who was not enthused to see him, but didn't kick him out like the day before.

"Hi Adam. How's it going today? Is the Physio doing anything for you yet?"

"Who knows? You tell me doc." Adam had little patience for David's chatter.

David noticed the framed photo.

"Casey bring you that photo?" David wanted to find out how Casey's visit went.

"Yup. Casey's going to stay at the house and take care of Rachel for me." Adam was not eager to let David know he was pushing Casey away.

"That's a surprise. I thought she would be returning to the cottage now that Robert is locked up." David hoped Adam would say more.

"Nope. So doc, what do you think my chances are of walking again? I know you're not an orthopedic surgeon, but maybe you've seen my type of injury at one time or another."

David was loathe to give Adam hope so he took a moment before answering.

"I don't recall seeing your injury in my time. But I believe there is usually room for hope given that your injury is incomplete. Even if it means walking with robotic limbs and such."

"Oh that sounds like fun. No, I mean really walking. On my own. My physio gal seems to think it may be possible."

"That's good Adam. She should know. Good luck then." David left thinking, *I need to let this play out and stop trying to control the situation. Let it go David!*

But David couldn't let it go. He kept seeing visions of himself and Casey flying home to the states together. His ring on her finger. *Damn! I need to get her out of that house.*

Chapter 52

Adam

Adam's mood had been getting lower all week. Being bed-ridden was hugely challenging for him. Casey dropped by regularly, but not daily. He continued to minimize their intimacy by not letting her stay long. But each time she left, honouring his wishes, he felt worse. He didn't realize he was pushing away the very person who could help him through this nightmare. By weeks end, he was noticeably depressed and the doctors were getting worried about his lack of will to try and his lack of progress in his physio sessions. They had discussed this fact with Adam and suggested he try an antidepressant which Adam outright refused. His doctor knew that David and Adam had a past, so he asked David if he would consider speaking to Adam about his depression. David went up to see Adam on the morning of his day off. After which he planned to go out and visit Casey.

"Hi Adam. I hear you're giving your physio girl a hard time these days."

"If you say so doc." Adam looked morose.

"Look, Adam. I know this is tough luck for you, but man, you've got to get a grip. Is there anything we can do to help you through this hard time?" David was sincere, at the moment, anyway.

"You know what doc? Stay away from Casey. That might make me feel better. Even if I'm not going to have her, the last thing I want to worry about, is her being with you! There! What do you say to that doc?" Adam thought, *what the hell, I may as well be honest. What have I got to lose now anyway?*

"Whoa...didn't expect that. I didn't even know Casey had broken off with you. That might explain your frame of mind though." David was glad he had dropped by now.

"Actually, what's going on between Casey and I is none of your business." Adam immediately regretted saying anything to David. *My mood swings are out of control all right.*"Just leave David." Adam turned his head away and closed his eyes.

"I will Adam. I suggest you start seeing a Psychologist to help you deal with this depression. That's all I'm going to say. At least, think about it."

David walked down the hall churning in turmoil. *I could so easily put Adam out of his misery and at the same time clinch my chances with Casey. Hey David, watch yourself. That would be cold blooded murder. Not if Adam gives up on life.* David argued with himself.

Within the hour David pulled into the driveway at the sea house. No sign of Casey but Adam's car was parked out front, which Casey had been driving since Adam's fall. There was also another vehicle. *I wonder who is here?* David thought possessively.

Casey opened the front door and looked surprised to see him there.

"Hi David. I didn't know you were coming by. I have a friend here but you're welcome to join us."

"Oh, sorry Casey. I should have called first. I don't want to impose." David hoped Casey would insist. She did.

"No, no it's fine. Really David. Come on in." Casey stepped aside so David could enter.

David entered the home and saw the older man sitting in the living room, Casey's landlord.

"Oh, hello Mr. O'Grady. It's been a long time. You're looking well." David walked over and shook the older man's hand.

"Aye, lad. As are ye. Oi was jes leavin' soon."

"Don't leave on my account." David said.

Mr. O'Grady said his goodbyes and Casey saw him to the door. He embraced Casey and she returned his hug. "Don't yer be a stranger!" He said, then left.

"How did you two get together?" David asked Casey.

"Well, as you know, he is my landlord at the cottage. He just called me one day and said we should have coffee. But he sure had a lot to tell me." She looked accusingly at David.

"Well, yes. He, of course, knew Brandy as she too rented the cottage from him."

"David, I do not understand why neither you nor Adam told me that Brandy had lived there. That at least, explained why you were so at home there. I feel duped, I have to ask, why the big secret?" Casey was annoyed with David.

"Okay, fair enough. Honestly, I didn't mention it for two reasons. One, I didn't want you to be even more uncomfortable knowing that Brandy died in that place. Two, I didn't want you to get mad at me for not telling you in the beginning. It just seemed after a while, it wasn't that important and you were already going through a lot. So try to cut me a little slack okay? It's a difficult thing to discuss with someone you are just getting to know."

Casey looked at David. He did seem genuine.

"I guess I can do that. I can understand how awkward that might have been." Casey relaxed a bit and calmed herself. But Mr. O'Grady had spoken poorly of David but hadn't had a chance to say why. He had warned Casey to use caution with David, so Casey was feeling guarded and confused. She would prefer it if David would leave, so she could think.

"Actually all this visiting has tired me out David. I didn't sleep well last night either, so would you mind if I asked you to leave so I can lie down?" Casey needed to be alone right now.

"Sure Casey, you need your rest, for sure." She did look very tired David thought.

After David left, Casey sat outside in a lounge chair, staring at the sea, deep in thought with Rachel resting at her feet.

Chapter 53

David, Casey & Adam

David had another restless night with very little sleep. *I'm beginning to obsess over Adam. This is not good. The urge to off that guy is getting the better of me. I need to focus on saving lives.*

The slippery slope of David's mercy killings was becoming self evident. He knew he was leaning into dark territory but didn't know how to stop himself.

I will go see Adam and check his level of depression. If he stays low, Casey may realize he's not for her. Slow down pal, do nothing you might live to regret, he cautioned himself.

Later that morning, when he neared Adam's room, he heard voices inside. Loud voices. One of them sounded like Casey's. He couldn't help but overhear.

"Forget it Casey! You cannot help me! I don't want to hear anymore of your miracle stories! Don't you see how torturous that is for me?" Adam yelled.

"But Adam, all I want is for you to have some hope! Is that asking too much? I cannot stand seeing you so hopeless!" Casey sounded panicky.

"That's exactly why you need to leave. Get out! Now!....Go!"

"Okay, okay. I'm going. The last thing I wanted to do was upset you." Casey entered the hallway. David had turned away from Adam's room and towards the nursing station. He turned back as he heard Adam's door open, then close. Casey was crying when she looked up and saw David.

"Casey, come with me." David quietly took her arm and guided her to an empty seating area close by. "I couldn't help but hear some of that. I'm sorry."

"Oh it's all so ridiculous David. I just brought Adam some online stories of people with similar spinal injuries to his, who are now, living full lives again and walking. I know how depressed he has become and just wanted him to have some hope." Casey wiped her eyes and blew her nose.

"Do you want some professional advice Casey?"

"Um, I'm not sure. Do I want to hear this?"

"Maybe not, but I think you need to hear it anyway. Adam is in a bad spot. He may or may not work his way out of it. Only time will tell. But you have more than just yourself now. It's imperative that you do not subject yourself to his moods, for the sake of your baby. All that stress sends excess hormones though your system which can affect the fetus. You know this already, I'm sure." David looked into Casey's wet eyes.

Casey looked down at her hands. "I know you are right, but knowing that, doesn't make it any easier, that's for sure. I just don't know what to do anymore."

"Maybe you need some counseling yourself...?" David suggested.

Casey gave him a half smile. "Perhaps I do. Here I am trying so hard to help Adam. Meanwhile it is affecting me, and not in a good way. I'm glad you happened along David. It's helpful to have someone to talk to about all this."

This was music to David's ears. All of it. "I'm glad I was there. You don't deserve to be treated like that, by anyone. Even a hurting patient. I was actually on this floor to check in on Adam, but I think I will leave it for now. I'm on duty shortly. Will you be okay?"

"Yes, I will." Casey was getting her balance back now. "I'm going to go do some sightseeing. I have barely had any time for that since I've arrived in Ireland."

They both went their separate ways. David with a bounce in his step. Casey with a steely determination to stay positive, for her baby's sake.

Chapter 54

Adam

After Casey left his room, in tears, Adam felt like a brute. *That exceptional woman did not deserve my bad mood thrust upon her. What is wrong with me? I can at least take a look at some of the material she brought in.*

Adam started reading about a new treatment out of the U.K. which seemed particularly interesting. It was published by the Independent Daily Edition and discussed some astonishing success with severe spinal cord injuries. He decided he would show it to Cynthia, his physio girl, when she came by and allowed himself to feel a tiny thread of hope.

I'm glad Casey isn't here right now. The last thing I want is to see hope in her eyes, only to see it replaced by despair and pity. I wish I didn't love her so damn much! This would be so much easier to bear if I could just let her go.

Cynthia came breezing in later that day. *All cheerful and annoying,* thought Adam. He shared the article with her.

"Finally, Adam! This is what I have been tryin' to tell yer. Sometimes there are nerves in there just waitin' fer the activity to spur 'em on. They can surprise yer. It starts out very slowly. Like when a woman is pregnant and she feels the very first flutter of 'movement' inside her womb. It's barely there, but it's the beginnin' of somethin'!" She said enthusiastically. Then she laughed."I guess that's not the best example, for a guy. But yer get my meanin'?"

"Sure." Adam was thinking about Casey's baby. He needed to talk with her, soon. He was starting to have hope.

Chapter 55

David

After his shift finished that day, David took a long walk, to think.

The hospital Clinical Director had pulled him aside that afternoon to speak with him, privately. The director informed him that the Bray family were going after the hospital for their daughter's sudden death and an internal investigation was underway. He wanted to give David the heads up, all staff involved would be called in for questioning.

David walked along the beautiful waterway at Liffey River downtown Dublin. He always found this walkway stunning, especially as the sun goes down and the city lights reflect on the water, as they did now. The scene soothed him.

Yes, I need Casey in my life and she needs me. There is only one way to make sure that happens. Adam must go. It's best for everyone. Time is critical now. Casey and I need to begin planning our return to the states before this investigation gets too far along. Just in case it doesn't go as I would expect.

David could feel the excitement of anticipation course through his body.

Best it happens tomorrow. Adam has been depressed and everyone knows he has refused treatment. It will look like cardiac failure and as depression can precede such an event, likely there will be no further investigation. Even if there is, it will look like heart failure. That medication I inject is never checked on toxicology screenings.

There...decision made. It feels good to stop mulling this over and over. Now I can just do it. With that uplifting thought, he stopped at a pub and went in to have a drink and relax.

Chapter 56

Adam

Adam was feeling euphoric now. After his session with Cynthia and discussion about the newspaper article, he felt better than he had in days and he told her that before she left.

"It's about bloody time. Ye bes be thankin' that girl!" Cynthia laughed.

Adam did want to thank Casey and apologize too. As soon as Cynthia left he called her cell, but no answer. Then he tried the house but only got the machine, so he left a message: "Hi Casey. It's me, Adam. I didn't want to wait another minute to tell you that I love you too! I am so, so sorry for being so stubborn. I promise it won't happen again. Well, at least, not for a while. I love you dammit and I want us to be together! I am going to do everything possible to get moving again. You and the baby are a powerful motivation for me. I hope you can forgive me Casey. Come and see me as soon as you're able. I want to plant one on you. Or maybe several, if you'll have them." Adam chuckled. It felt so good to have faith again that he and Casey could get through anything together. "See you soon, I hope!"

Chapter 57

Casey

While Casey was out touring around the city she made up her mind to be optimistic about Adam. She parked the car whenever something caught her eye, like a colourful little shop or a park with vibrant flowers. It seemed there were bright colours everywhere. She loved it. Her mood had been improving all afternoon and she constantly sent Adam loving thoughts of positivity.

Parking was tricky for her though, given the right sided steering wheel. *The only way to fix that problem is practice and more practice. I have a hope that I may be living here a while.* She cheerfully mused.

After exploring Dublin she drove back to the sea house before dark. The rolling green hills filled her spirit with hope. The distant sea affirmed her belief that anything is possible.

When she opened the front door, Rachel came bounding to see her. They headed outside first, then came back inside where Casey started foraging for food. She didn't see the blinking message light on the house phone until later that night, when she came out to the kitchen, in the dark, to get a glass of water.

As she listened to Adam's message, she started to tear up. Tears of relief. She could barely believe her ears and played it again. Then a third time.

Thank you God. My prayers have been answered. Thank you!

She put her hands on her belly.

"Okay little one, it looks like you are going to have a wonderful Daddy. I cannot wait for you two to meet."

Casey's joy filled her being. She had never felt so complete in her life and could barely wait to see Adam in the morning. She couldn't quit smiling as she poured her glass of water and headed back to her room.

Chapter 58

Robert

The doctor looked somber as he entered Robert's cell in the jail. It had taken a few days for the results of all the medical tests he had undergone.

"Hiya Doc. What's the word?" Robert would have preferred that a guard just give him the all clear. This visit made him nervous.

"I have some bad news. You have a brain tumour. It is pressing on your frontal lobe and could quite possibly explain your recent troubles. It can cause mood swings, inability to reason and aggression, among other things. We need to operate as soon as possible. Those headaches of yours are getting worse and that pressure needs to be relieved. Brain surgery is always serious, so I suggest you get your affairs in order, as much as you can, before the operation. We will be moving you to the hospital this evening in preparation for the first available time slot for surgery, likely in a few days. You will go under Garda supervision of course. Do you have any questions?"

"I think my mind is a blank Doc. But I need to write a letter to my wife. Can you get someone to find me paper and an envelope?" Robert could not process all this. He just knew he wanted to write a letter to Casey.

"I'm sure that can be arranged. You will be transported to the hospital within he next few hours. I will see you there and can answer any questions you may have in the morning. Okay? I am sorry to have to give you this news Mr. Paterson."

"Thank you anyway." Robert wanted him to go so he could think. *Brain tumour? Who would have thought that? Maybe this will be my 'get out of jail free' card. Who knows? I just need to tell Casey how much I love her. If I die, so be it.*

The guard returned with a few sheets of paper, an envelope and a pen for Robert which he handed over.

"Hey, I'm sorry man. Just heard. That's a rotten break."

Robert sat down, headache raging and started writing. He had no idea what to say, he just wrote.

Dear Casey,

I need you to know that I have a brain tumour. Surgery will be done in the next few days. But the doctor has explained to me that my behaviour the past while could have been caused by the tumour. He says mood swings, aggressive behaviour and poor reasoning can be brought on by this type of growth.

He also told me to get my affairs in order, in case I don't make it through surgery.

I want to tell you how sorry I am for all that I have done Casey. It drove me crazy having you leave me like that. I could not wrap my head around it. I felt like I was losing my mind and now I know I was. But brain tumour or not, that is a lousy excuse for what I put you through. I am very SORRY.

Please forgive me. I understand if you cannot, I wouldn't blame you. But as I have nothing left to lose I must tell you I love you. I have since the day I met you. You saved me and I will always be so glad you were in my life.

I also have to tell you that I lied to you. I was married before. I had just gotten out of jail shortly before I met you, for assault. I was too afraid to tell you. I know it's a lot to ask but if you could possibly forgive me before I go under the knife, it would mean a lot.

If you can't, I understand. Just know that I will always love you and if you ever reconsider and come back to me, I promise to always put you first Casey. I have learned what a self centred prick I can be, at times. But by living without you, I now understand what it takes to not just love someone, but to actually show your love through your actions.

You, of all people know what my upbringing did to me, but I never really told you how bad it was. I was ashamed to be in such a lousy family so I didn't share a whole lot. You always said we are here on earth to learn many lessons, well I feel like I am. I am sorry that you got hurt by me, before I figured that out.

I am going to a hospital in Dublin tonight so I will write the name of the hospital on the envelope and have the Garda deliver it to you.

Hope to see you but either way, I wish you a good life from here on.

Yours Always,

Love Robert

"Well now it's up to you Casey." Robert sat quietly thinking about the bombshell just delivered to him.

Chapter 59

David, Casey & Adam

The following morning David headed for Adam's room. He had a potent medication in his pocket and his adrenaline was pumping. The thinnest infant needle was always his syringe of choice. So small, the entry site was nearly undetectable. His drug of choice was Digoxin. It was used regularly in the hospital to regulate heart rhythm and never routinely included in a toxicology screening. The right amount mimics cardiac failure, so seldom would there be any suspicion. It was the same procedure he always used. David felt that familiar surge of anticipation when he knew he was acting for the greater good.

The sooner this is over, the sooner Casey and I can be together, he told himself.

As he entered Adam's room, he saw Adam was still sleeping.

"This is perfect." David whispered. He pulled out the syringe, pumped it and leaned over Adam's sleeping torso.

"David! What are you doing?" Casey abruptly spoke as she walked into the room.

David nearly jumped into the air. He quickly hid the syringe as he turned to smile at Casey. Adam woke up then.

"What's going on here? Did I miss anything?" His eyes went to Casey who quickly came over to him. She took Adam's hand and turned to David.

"What are you doing here David?" Casey asked.

"I just wanted make sure Adam was okay. He was so down yesterday, I was concerned." David lied. "I can leave you two alone now, if you want." Giving Casey his warmest smile, thinking: *This will have to happen another day. Those two look pretty friendly though.*

Casey looked at him quizzically, thinking to herself, something isn't right here. But she turned her attention back to Adam, as David left the room.

"Adam..." Casey was suddenly shy. "I..was...so happy to get your message last night. Is it really true?"

Adam laughed out loud. "Yes it's true, I love you Casey. I am such a fool! Can you ever forgive me? I'm a guy. We seldom get it right. You must forgive me!" Adam was not going to hold back anymore.

"Of course. I love you too. How could I possibly not forgive you? Adam, I am just so thankful that you finally get it. We can do this together, right?"

Adam pulled Casey towards him and held her tight. "No kisses until I brush my teeth!" She laughed. "I'm good with that Adam."

They were both giggling like school children. Adam put both his hands on her cheeks. He looked into her eyes.

"Casey, with you by my side I feel like I can do anything, including conquer my injury. I can't promise you I will walk again, but I can promise you I will not give up easily. The good news is that once I make up my mind, I can get things done. The bad news is, I can be one stubborn son of a gun! Do you think you can handle that?" Adam was more serious now.

"You bet! Psychology is my first love Adam. You were meant for me." Casey chuckled. "Besides I can personally assure you, that

I am no walk in the park either. I may seem perfect, but am far from it." She grinned at him.

"No worries, Lassie.." Adam was putting on his best Irish accent now.

"Yer perfect fer himself!" With that he pulled Casey close and held her like he would never let her go.

Chapter 60

Casey

*L*ater that afternoon, while Adam was in Physio, Casey grabbed a bite to eat in the cafeteria. She was surprised to see Officer Delaney approach her.

"Do you mind if I join you?" Officer Delaney had on her poker face.

"Sure, have a seat. What's going on?" Casey had not expected to hear anymore news on the case against Robert for a while.

"Here. Robert asked us to pass this letter on to you." The officer watched Casey closely.

"Is this proper or legal? Should I even open this?" Casey felt guarded. *Now what is Robert up to?*

"You are under no obligation to read it. But I am under obligation to tell you that Robert has just been diagnosed with a brain tumour and is scheduled for surgery as soon as possible. In fact, he was admitted to this hospital last night. This diagnosis could affect the case against him, in more ways than one. He may not make it through surgery, so I suspect that could be the reason for his letter. Read it or not, you will be required to hand it over as evidence in the case. I'm sorry to deliver this news Casey."

Casey was silent as she looked at the envelope being held out to her. This felt like one of those moments in life which hits you unexpectedly and sends shockwaves through your brain and body. You never forget that moment. She took the letter. *Why am I so devastated? How can I still care what happens to Robert? Damn him! I do not want to feel sorry for him, but I do. Just when Adam and I are getting back on track, now this?*

'Part of me just wants to give this letter back and never read it. But how can I do that when I know Robert may not live beyond his operation? Brain tumour? He has had headaches for a long time but they never found anything. Then he just quit going in to see the doctors and decided to live with them." Casey said and looked at Officer Delaney. "Do I want to read this?"

"If you're asking for my advice, then given the circumstances I think you need to read it. If for no other reason, that you can live with yourself after, in case he dies."

"Yes, I know you are right. I should probably be alone. In fact, I think I'll take it to the Chapel and read it there."

"Sure, go ahead. I'll walk with you and wait outside the chapel until you are finished with it. No rush."

In the Chapel Casey seated herself, said a prayer then opened the envelope. She began reading. Soon there were tears streaming down her face. When she got to the line asking for her forgiveness, prior to his surgery, she froze. *Oh my God, what do I do? I never wanted to see him again. Yet, he was my husband and for a few years I loved him. I have discovered that love never really dies, it just changes. I love Adam now. Poor, sweet, injured Adam. Yet, I still care for Robert, especially now that his behaviour has a possible explanation. Yet he was so cruel. Dear God, please guide me.*

Casey finished reading the letter. She took a deep breath and began to feel calm. *Yes, I love Adam. But the truth is I have compassion for Robert, in spite of all that has happened. I'm carrying his child too. Do I dare tell him? It would make him so happy. But it would also create complications down the road, if he lives. Doesn't the Bible say 'The truth shall set you free? Again, what can I live with? Robert dying and never knowing he has brought a child into this world or Robert living and wanting to be a father to that child?*

Casey left her pew, walked to the alter and got down on her knees. She prayed for a long time. After, she returned to the pew and sat quietly.

She remembered reading about a Traditional Japanese Art form called KINTSUGI which was the ancient practice of mending broken China with embedded gold seams, creating an exquisite piece of art. Rather than discarding that which is damaged, one embraces it and artfully works with it to highlight the cracks while transforming the whole into something of greater value. The Philosophy that brokenness can be mended to create something more precious, moved Casey's heart.

Embrace the imperfect and find the unique beauty within it, she reflected. *My broken life can be mended and my shattered dreams need not remain shattered. I know what I must do now and I trust that however my future unfolds, I can create the life I hold in my dreams.*

She stood up, made the sign of the cross and walked out of the Chapel to find Officer Delaney.

The End

🍀 If you want to continue reading Casey's ongoing odyssey, look for Book 2 in this series titled STEADFAST in Spring 2020

If you enjoyed this book and want to be notified by email of the release date of STEADFAST, simply drop me an email and I will keep you posted.

My email: writersneverstop@gmail.com

Made in the USA
San Bernardino, CA
12 January 2020